BIRDING IN BREWSTER SQUARE

Narielle Living

Cactus Mystery Press
an imprint of Blue Fortune Enterprises, LLC

For information contact :
Blue Fortune Enterprises, LLC
Cactus Mystery Press
P.O. Box 554
Yorktown, VA 23690
http://blue-fortune.com

Book and Cover design by Blue Fortune Enterprises, LLC
Edited by Lion by the Tail

ISBN: 978-1-948979-77-1
First Edition: February 2022

Dedication

To those who have lost a loved one and are grieving.
You are not alone.

TITLES BY NARIELLE LIVING

Brewster Square Series Cozy Mysteries:
Madness in Brewster Square
Birding in Brewster Square
Searching in Brewster Square

Paranormal Mysteries:
Signs of the South
Revenge of the Past

Holiday Books:
Christmas in Virginia

ACKNOWLEDGEMENTS

Dear Reader,

Welcome to the second Brewster Square mystery! I hope you have as much fun reading this as I had writing it. A few notes about Brewster Square. People have asked me the location of the town of Brewster Square. It is entirely fictitious, but I have taken elements of Wooster Square in New Haven and the small town of Branford on the shoreline to create this place. Occasionally I throw in landmarks that have nothing to do with either place.

In addition, the search and rescue team mentioned in this book, Connecticut Shoreline Search and Rescue (CSSAR), is a figment of my imagination. There is, however, a group called Connecticut Canine Search and Rescue (CCSAR). They are a dedicated group of volunteers who work with their dogs to locate missing persons. For more information on this group, check out their website at ccsar.org.

Thank you to my editor, Amy, at Lion by the Tail. Her grace and wisdom made this a better book.

Big thanks go to my family and friends for the support they've given me through the years. And thank you to my sweet search dog, Sonny, who sits with me while I'm writing or fiddling and who loves going out to search for people.

I love you all,

Narielle

Chapter One

Baby Danny, who was only one and a half years old, didn't mean to ruin things for me. It just worked out that way. His contribution to my weekend became the start of something bigger. Much bigger and much worse. But I couldn't blame a toddler.

My plans had been in place for weeks. I'd packed my suitcase and left it with my boyfriend, Stanley, and my dog would be staying with my brother. Everything was set, except I was running late. I told my brother I had to leave work at two o'clock, but at a quarter to two he asked me to shelve the new merchandise at the store. Apparently, the job had to be done *right this second*.

I should blame my brother for how it started. Not because of the work he asked me to do—yes, it had been last minute, and yes, it could have waited—but because of his bizarre food issues. My brother and sister-in-law always gave that poor, sweet child some type of foul-smelling organic food that any normal human being wouldn't feed to their fish.

I loved my nephew; I did. But I made sure to never, ever pick him up right after he'd eaten, as it was only a matter of time before he'd regurgitate his all-natural, organic, GMO-free, antibiotic-free, taste-free superfood. The child was incapable of keeping a meal down, and who could blame him.

I'd stopped by my brother's house after finishing at the store. I thought I'd deliver the day's mail, which wouldn't take long. But without thinking, I picked up Baby Danny. And just like that, my new aqua blue silk blouse, meant to complement my curly red hair and make me look sophisticated, was toast. My curly hair wasn't looking so good, either.

I thrust the baby back to Giuseppe and grabbed a towel. After trying and failing to get most of the organic cement off me, I gave up. I'd have to fix myself once I got to Stanley's house. I said a quick goodbye, patted my dog on the tummy (not that he cared, he had his toy to play with), and hustled down the street and around the corner to Stanley's.

"Ready?" he asked and slammed the hatch closed.

"Almost. I need my suitcase for a minute."

Stanley shook his head. "You'll have to wait until we get to my parents' house. I've arranged the china on top of our luggage and strapped it down so nothing moves or breaks. Everything is perfectly packed."

Stanley's mother had insisted that Stanley bring his grandmother's fine china with him when he visited. The dishes had sat in storage at Stanley's house for years, but for some reason, she needed them *right this second.* Now boxes of china rested on top of my suitcase in the hatchback of the car. The suitcase that contained clean clothes.

"But I need a shirt." And a mirror. Or maybe it was better not to know. "I'll just go home for a quick—"

Stanley looked at his watch. "Ava, we have to leave now so we don't hit rush hour traffic." He glanced over at me. "Besides, you're fine. You're already wearing a shirt." He squinted, and I knew he'd seen the stain. He was too polite to say anything. Or he didn't want to be late.

"I need to get in my suitcase. Or I could go home and grab another shirt." I gave him what I thought was my sweetest smile, but it must have been more of a grimace because it didn't work. He just shook his head.

I tried again. "It won't take that long." Clearly Stanley did not understand. I couldn't show up at his parents' house looking and smelling like this. "Five minutes."

Stanley ignored my plea and climbed into the car. He sat and waited. *I don't even get the door opened for me? He won't get my suitcase or let me go home and now he won't open the door?* I stomped over to the car, threw myself into the passenger seat, and slammed the door as hard as I could. Childish, yes, but I couldn't help it.

And that's when I started to have a bad feeling about this weekend.

I leaned my head against the headrest and closed my eyes. This was not part of my plan. I did not look glamorous. I did not smell pretty. I certainly wouldn't make a good first impression, and I wanted Stanley's family to welcome and accept me. Instead, they'd probably ask me to use the service entrance and help clean the ashes out of the fireplace.

If they had a service entrance.

To be honest, I didn't know much about Stanley's family. I knew he had a sister, Victoria, and his father was a professor at a prestigious college in New London. I wasn't sure what his mother did. I also recalled something about an older brother that nobody talked about.

After twenty minutes of driving, I opened my eyes and stared out at the plant life. Green leaves and blooming flowers—not just those yellow chrysanthemums that signaled colder weather was almost, but not quite, gone—dotted the Interstate 95 corridor. Tulips congregated in full force, and soon the lilacs would burst with fragrance. At this time of year, after an interminable winter and a halfhearted spring, any sign of life was more than welcome in Connecticut.

Trucks and cars whipped past us, only to brake when someone in the left lane insisted on going the speed limit. Stanley stayed in the right lane, cruising at a steady sixty-two miles an hour.

"Do you want to listen to the radio?" he asked.

"Sure." Music might calm my nerves.

He wrinkled his nose. "What's that smell? Did something get wet in the car?"

The smell was my baby-puke shirt and hair. I could've mentioned that this was the result of his insistence that we leave without him digging out my suitcase. But I didn't want to whine any more than I already had before we left. We were still new enough in our relationship that I felt like I always needed to look good, a feat I was failing miserably at the moment. A wave of embarrassment flooded my body. Just as quickly, annoyance replaced shame. Stanley hadn't helped the situation. At all.

"What station do you want to listen to?" I asked. Changing the subject might distract us both. I reached up and pulled my hair back, wondering if I should put it in a ponytail to hide the stringy look I now sported.

"Maybe I left the car windows open, and it rained," he said. "Sometimes I forget to check them."

Was he really that dense, or was he trying to make me feel better? Neither option cheered me. "Indeed," I said, remaining noncommittal. "I don't know what you usually listen to. Classic Rock? Alternative?"

Stanley didn't even hesitate as he reached over and flipped on the radio. "Talk radio. Love those shows."

I settled into my seat and stared out the window again. It was going to be a long ride.

Our trip lasted fifty minutes. To get to Stonington, Connecticut, we traveled directly up the highway to the state's northeastern area from our little town of Brewster Square. Stonington was next to Mystic, the town famous in the '80s because of the Julia Roberts movie. Most people remember Mystic now for the shopping and tourist attractions.

Stanley's parents lived in a quiet suburban area, a tree-lined neighborhood with upscale houses. He pulled into the driveway of an elegant colonial with a perfectly manicured lawn. I sat up and smoothed my hair. I'd surreptitiously put the window down on my side for the last fifteen minutes of the ride, hoping the Baby Danny vomit smell would dissipate enough for me to meet the folks and get changed. Honestly, couldn't my brother be like the rest of the world and feed his kid regular food instead of toxic strength super-yuck?

Stanley reached over and squeezed my hand. "I'm glad you're here, Ava. This means a lot to me."

Stanley had invited me to come with him to his parents' anniversary dinner a couple of months ago. We'd just started dating, and I'd been super excited that it was a sign our relationship was going somewhere. Even though we were still in the beginning stages—where everything was still new and wonderful—I felt like Stanley and I had something special. I pushed away the memory of him not listening to me earlier.

Ping.

I rifled through my purse, trying to find my cell phone.

Where R U?

"Who is it?" Stanley asked.

"Oliver," I answered. I didn't want to tell him, but I had no choice. Stanley and I agreed always to be honest with each other, no matter what.

Stonington. Dinner w/ S parents.

Stanley let out a sigh. "The investigation is over. What does he want?"

Stanley was referring to the investigation into who had killed Ethel, a universally despised Brewster Square resident. I'd been unfortunate enough to find her body and couldn't stand the thought that her killer might evade justice. At the time, I took it upon myself to investigate—caving to the demands from my brother that I find out what happened—and almost got myself killed by two people in the process.

When will u be back? U can have dinner w/ me.

"He wants to have dinner?" I couldn't help that my sentence came out like a question. Oliver and I did not have the best of relationships. He thought I was nosy, and I thought he wasn't doing his job. We sort of patched things up by the time we caught the killer, but I wasn't sure why he was asking me to dinner.

"Didn't you have coffee with him already this week?" Stanley asked, sounding petulant.

"It wasn't like we arranged a date and I dressed up and met him. He brought me coffee when I had to work late on Tuesday, that's all."

"With food, right?"

I nodded, not sure what food had to do with anything. "I took him around Brewster Square last week, but that's because I thought he needed a history lesson. If he's going to work in this part of the world, he needs to understand what happened here and what people are like."

"Are you the Brewster Square ambassador now?"

I didn't like Stanley's tone, but I understood. He'd always felt threatened by Oliver, a former DEA agent who could pose for any month of the calendar.

"I'm sorry," he said. "I don't know what got into me."

"We agreed we'd be honest with each other, and I'm telling you what's going on," I said. "I'm not going to do something behind your back."

Stanley sighed and pushed his floppy blond hair back from his face. "I know. Please bear with me. Being here is… you know." He gestured to the house in front of us.

I wasn't sure where he was going with that statement, so I waited while he seemed to drift into space. Finally, he said, "Being here brings up bad memories. I don't mean to take it out on you."

I considered exploring the thought further, especially since I had no idea what he was talking about. Bad memories? I could guess all day, but maybe I could get him to talk about it. I wanted to know more about Stanley.

"I'm always here if you—"The ping of my cell phone distracted me again. *Dinner?*

A flush crept up my face. Yes, I wanted to know more about Stanley. But I also wanted to learn more about Oliver. Did that mean I was nosy, or did it mean something else?

I didn't have time to think about it because a group of people had gathered in the driveway. I sent back a hasty *yes* to Oliver, got out of the car, and tried to project an air of confidence.

"Mom, Dad… good to see you both," Stanley said as he hugged his parents. He ignored the other two people standing to the side. "I'd like you to meet my… friend, Ava. Ava, this is my mother, Birdie."

Birdie was a small woman with a sharp face who looked a little like her name. Her face lit up in a smile when she saw me, but cynic that I am, I couldn't tell if the smile was genuine or not. "Beatrice," she said. She extended her hand to me and stared at my shirt.

"Nice to meet you." I angled myself so that my arm covered the front of my shirt, but I knew I wasn't fooling anyone. And what was with him calling me his friend? Hadn't he told his parents about me?

"We all call her Birdie," Stanley said and beamed at his mother. That was fine for Stanley and his family, but the jury was still out on what I'd be calling this woman, especially since I was a *friend*. "And this is my father, Chase."

Clearly Stanley's boyish good looks came from his dad. Slightly taller than average, Chase had the same bright eyes and dimples. He stepped forward and bowed his head as he clasped my hand in both of his. "It is a pleasure to meet you, my dear. Welcome."

"Thank you."

A silence hovered around us for a moment. *I'm guessing that's his sister standing off to the side with someone who just crash-landed from the sixties.* The woman wore a white lace shirt buttoned to her neck and a long black skirt with a slit up to her thigh. She resembled a Jane Austen character gone bad.

Stanley cleared his throat. "Hey Vicky, nice to see you."

"It's Tory now, remember?" She sneered at us, but I wasn't sure why. She might've been a fashion mystery to me, but the man standing next to her sent shivers of apprehension up my spine. He looked like he had just jumped off the acid-dropping train with his flowing linen shirt, faded blue jeans, and love beads. He reminded me of someone I couldn't quite place.

"Ava, this is… Tory," Stanley said, staring at his sister as if he'd never met her before.

"Lovely to meet you, Evie."

"It's Ava," Stanley corrected.

Tory gestured to the man standing next to her. As he looked at me, my stomach dropped, and I felt sick. Tory wrapped herself around him. "This is my partner, Valdorn."

I didn't want to be sick, not in front of Stanley's parents. But this guy, Tory's boyfriend—Valdorn—I knew him.

Chapter Two

It's not like you actually know him, Stanley had said later that night. True, I'd argued, I'd never met him, but I knew who and what he was. I knew his type: the all-organic, love-peace-and-poison-type. I'd almost been killed by one. And this guy set my internal alarms ringing. Although possibly my alarms weren't working as well as they should. Lately they'd go off for no apparent reason.

Saturday morning greeted me with the sun shining brightly through the bedroom window. I'd spent the night tossing and turning on the twin bed in a room with no curtains, so at the first sign of daybreak, I knew it was over. I gave up any illusion of sleep.

I reached for my phone to check the time. No point in getting up so early I woke everyone else. Last night kept replaying in my mind. The look on Valdorn's face. The adoring way Tory twined herself around him, like a cat around a can of tuna.

"She's always had bad taste in guys," Stanley had said last night. "Just ignore him. I'm pretty sure this one will go away, too. All the others did."

A glance at my phone told me a text had come in.

Call when u r back.

I only hesitated a moment. Sure, it was early, but that's the beauty of sending a text; it can be easily ignored.

Met someone last night.

I pushed send before I finished the thought. *Why do I do that?* As I typed a clarification, an answering text came in.

Thought u already had a boyfriend.

I smiled. He was awake. Good. Stanley wouldn't be happy about me talking to Oliver at six o'clock in the morning, but I wasn't going to worry about it. After all, I'd tried to talk to Stanley about Valdorn last night. And he'd dismissed my fears.

Not boyfriend material. This guy reminded me of the crazies. Scared me. I knew Oliver would understand. After about fifteen seconds, the phone buzzed in my hand.

"You didn't have to call. I'm sure you're still waking up," I said.

"No, I've been up," Oliver answered. "I just finished my workout. Are you okay?"

I tried not to think about people who got up at dawn to work out. "I'm fine. No worries." I stopped talking for a moment. I needed to be honest about my feelings. "This guy, he sort of threw me, you know? The fear came for no reason."

"I've had that happen." Oliver's soft voice comforted me. "Like I told you after the whole thing went down, this could take a while for you to get over. Some people have flashbacks or irrational fears. Be patient with yourself. What was it about this guy that spooked you?"

I loved that he didn't dismiss what I was feeling but got straight to the problem. "It's the way he's dressed. Like a hippie, in a trying-to-be-cool fashion sense. But not cool." I took a breath to stop babbling.

"How did you meet him?"

"Stanley's sister. He's her boyfriend, I guess. And he's got a weird name, too. He reminded me of all those people acting oddly because they'd been eating that organic yuck from Debbee-with-two-e's." I couldn't get air into my lungs. Was it because of what happened in March or the strangeness of talking with Oliver so early in the morning that made me go on and on? Whatever. *Calm down, Ava.*

"Where are you?" he asked.

"Stanley's house," I said. "I mean, his parents' house. He grew up here. I don't know where Valdorn came from, though." Not important information, but sometimes I couldn't stop talking about inane things. "Nice neighborhood, real suburban, you know?"

"Mmm," he said. I had no idea what that meant, so I waited. "Did you say Valdorn? Is that the hippie boyfriend?"

"Yes. Weird name and all."

"And you'll be home soon?"

"Sunday. We're here for an anniversary dinner. But I don't think there's going to be many people, just family. I'm not even sure how long they've been married. I guess I should ask, right?" Again, I couldn't seem to stop babbling words that didn't matter. The fact that Oliver didn't comment made me wonder how often I did this and if he was simply used to me talking endlessly.

"Will you be with Stanley all weekend?" *What a weird question.* I wasn't sure what difference it made to Oliver, so I didn't answer. Sometimes I'm stubborn like that.

"What's going on with you?" I asked. "Are you finally feeling like you fit in here in Connecticut?" Oliver moved to Brewster Square after working as a DEA agent in Arizona. I discovered, after running an internet check on him—I Googled his name—that a criminal had kidnapped his wife. She'd never been found and eventually pronounced dead. Oliver never talked about it, other than to hint that I couldn't understand what happened. I understood enough to know he'd come to the East Coast to escape his past, and he'd downgraded to detective at a small-town police station because it was easier than sticking around Arizona and its constant reminders. I often wondered if he regretted his choice. I wondered what I'd do. I wondered if he still loved her. But it was none of my business.

"Do me a favor," he said. "Try to stay close to Stanley all weekend."

What the heck was he talking about? "I don't know what you mean," I said.

"I mean, don't go running off with people you don't know. Don't take chances. Stay safe. Be smart."

O-kay. Did he know something I didn't? Because he'd said that the kind of thing all the time during Ethel's murder investigation. "Oliver, what's going on?"

"Nothing. It's just that if you do things to stay safe, it will make you feel better," he said. "This hippie guy sort of freaked you out, right?"

I nodded, even though he couldn't see me.

"Since you're not feeling safe based on past experiences, do things that will make you feel proactive in your personal protection," he said. "Use some of those situational awareness techniques I taught you. That will go a long way toward peace of mind."

It made sense, even though his wording was kind of weird. "I'll do that. I've gotta go because I seriously need some coffee."

"Call me when you get home," he said.

"Sure." I disconnected, stretched, and went downstairs in hopes of finding a coffee maker or luck be with me—a Keurig. I figured everyone was still asleep and didn't see the point in making an entire pot of coffee if it'd be nothing but sludge in a couple of hours. On the far side of the kitchen, a set of French doors opened onto a patio, where a still figure stood at the edge of the terrace—Stanley's father. He held a pair of binoculars to his face. I guess I wasn't the only early riser.

Is he okay? I'd never seen anyone stand so motionless. He dropped the binoculars, attached by a cord around his neck, and picked up a small, spiral-bound notebook on the wrought iron table next to him and started writing.

I sighed. I had an idea of his outdoor pursuit despite never personally participating in this type of activity. I didn't want to interrupt his birdwatching, but if I went into the kitchen to make coffee, he'd see me. Nothing I could do about that, so I decided to take control of the situation.

I quietly opened the door and stepped out into the cool morning air. Chase looked up, saw me, and smiled. "Hi, sorry to bother you," I said. "I'm making coffee. Would you like some?"

"That would be great. There's a single-cup coffee maker on the counter, and the pods are in the drawer underneath. Thanks."

I tried to be unobtrusive and leave since I knew he was probably looking for toucans or something. Isn't that what birders did? Tried to find exotic species?

Chase put the binoculars up to his eyes again and kept talking. "I understand you live in Brewster Square, too."

Crap. I wanted nothing more than to get inside and drink a cup of coffee. "Yes, around the corner from Stanley. I live in one of the buildings that face the Green."

Chase nodded. "It's a lovely town. I know some people who live in Brewster Square. You may know them."

I stared off into the bushes in the backyard, wondering if he actually saw any birds. I sure as heck didn't. I didn't hear any birdsong, either. "I grew up there, so I know a lot of people. I'm not sure I'd know your friends, though. Have they lived there long?"

Chase put the binoculars down and turned to me. *Maybe he'll write my name down in his bird book as if I'm the strange species he saw this morning.*

"Yes, as a matter of fact, they have. Do you know Win Thurgood?"

CHAPTER THREE

The fact that I did not like Win Thurgood shouldn't have any bearing on what I thought of Stanley's father. So what if they were friends? So what if Win Thurgood was a stuck-up, pompous jerk-wad who happened to be the father of my BFF's boyfriend?

Chase slanted a sideways look at me. "I haven't seen Win in quite some time," he added. He fiddled with the strap around his neck, probably wishing he could get back to watching birds and regretting starting this painful conversation with some woman Stanley brought home. "Do you know him?"

Couldn't Chase see by my awkward body posture that I didn't want to talk about Win? But I had to answer the question. Stanley's dad deserved a certain level of respect, at least according to what my parents had taught me.

I kept it simple. "Yes, I know him. But I know his son better."

Chase's face lit up with a smile. "Fred's a great kid. I've known him since he was a baby. Hard to believe he's all grown-up now."

While it was nice to stand outside in the early morning hours and make small talk with Stanley's father, my pressing need for coffee was making its presence known. The beginnings of a headache pulsed behind my eyes, and a fog-like sensation crept into my head. I mumbled some words of agreement, unable to articulate anything more.

Chase nodded and winked. "Why don't you go inside and get your coffee? I'll be in soon. I just want to see if the rose-breasted grosbeak is going to find her way back here."

I'd never heard of a rose-breasted grosbeak, but I knew the key word in Chase's sentence was *grosbeak*. And when you broke that word down, you had the word *beak*—obviously a bird of some sort. *Nice detective skills, Ava.* One of these days I'd put those skills to good use.

I went inside and brewed two cups of dark roast, then brought one out to Chase before returning to the kitchen. I sat at the table and cradled the liquid gold. Exactly what I needed. Halfway through my second cup, Chase came in and poured himself another cup, too.

I noted his movements, trying not to be too obvious. He was neat and assured and moved with an economy of motion.

"Stanley mentioned you teach at the local college," I said. "What do you teach?"

"Avian biology," he said. "As well as Quantitative Phylogenetics and Principles of Systematic Entomology. I'm thinking of cutting back on my course load, though."

"I don't blame you. Those are some heavy-hitting classes." I had no idea what the heck he was talking about. Time to change the subject. "Do you have good students?"

A peculiar look crossed his face. "What makes you ask that question?"

"When I was in college, I'd have these great classes, and sometimes it was like the students didn't care at all, even if it was their major. They'd goof off and try to cheat, or they were downright rude to everyone in the room, including the professor. But sometimes I'd have classes where everyone was bright, engaged, and working hard. And I never figured out why there was such a difference, except that the students themselves were all different."

He gave a quick nod. "Exactly what I've tried to tell Birdie! I don't know until I start teaching the class how it will go for the semester. You would think that after all these years of teaching the same subjects, I would know what to expect, but that isn't the case at all."

A silence fell over us. I sat and drank more coffee. Sometimes silence can be comfortable, but when you're sitting in your boyfriend's parents' kitchen in your pajamas with a man you just met, well, sometimes silence is… not comfortable.

I stood, stammered, "Thanks for the coffee," and fled to my room. Hopefully the rest of the weekend would get easier.

My expectations for the anniversary party were nonexistent, since I knew nothing beyond what Stanley had told me. And Stanley had only told me what to wear. He was good about that; he had a sense of fashion for different occasions, which is what made his refusal to let me change my shirt the day before perplexing. At least this time I'd be appropriately dressed.

I didn't know where the party was happening, who'd be there, or how many people I didn't know would be there. I was curious about Stanley's family. Nobody seemed all that excited about the night's events. Birdie went about her day, a bit distracted and fluttery, Chase left to play golf, and Tory secreted herself in a darkened family room—blinds drawn and curtains closed—with her weirdo boyfriend.

I mulled over my anxiety about Valdorn. I reasoned that my feelings had less to do with Valdorn the person and more my one bad experience with a New Age-y, woo-woo person. Their similarities didn't mean that every person like Valdorn was out to kill me. *Giuseppe never tried to hurt me.*

Beyond the usual brother stuff, that is.

I worked at Scentsations, the aromatherapy store Giuseppe owned in Brewster Square. My brother believed in all things alternative: health food, auras, aliens, and ghosts. Because of those beliefs, as well as his ghost-hunting group, I'd gotten caught up in an investigation that made me harbor an extreme distrust of all people who claimed to see spirits and auras and such. Never mind the fact that I'd also seen a ghost. I attributed that little moment of insanity to pure adrenaline.

After all, there's no such thing as ghosts, right?

The dinner took place at the Stonington Inn, a large and imposing stone structure. Colonial-era lanterns graced the immense front door, creating the feel of a different time, perhaps a place where dinner was had by candlelight. Inside, the tables and settings reflected elegance. Muted conversations swirled throughout the large dining room as waitstaff moved soundlessly from table to table, pouring water and carrying large trays of decorative dishes plated for presentation as much as taste. I'd heard about this place but had never dined here. I assumed the prices matched the look.

The family had reserved a long table that seated twenty-five people. I only knew Stanley and his parents. And his sister. And, of course, Valdorn, but I tried not to think of him. Everyone else resembled Chase: slightly past middle age, dressed in conservative blazers and khakis, and subdued. It wasn't just their appearances that clued me in. Conversations revolved around thirteenth-century Byzantine politics and revisionist history of the Jacobite rising of 1715. Some talk of a birding and wildlife festival also made circulations, but it was in Virginia and didn't happen until October. Most everyone at the table seemed to be making plans to attend. I assumed an interest in wildlife recreation was the common thread among Chase's colleagues.

Dinner was pleasant enough. I managed to participate in parts of the conversation, although nothing scintillating. I resisted the urge to question Stanley why his relatives—aunts, uncles, and cousins—weren't at the dinner. I didn't want to make him or his parents uncomfortable on their anniversary. There'd be a better time to dig for answers.

I thought I heard some whispers related to Chase a few times, but when I tried to enter the conversation, people simply stopped talking. Snatches of the phrase, "I don't know what he'll do next," floated by, followed by quite a few tsks and several shaking heads. *Wonder what Stanley's father got himself into.*

Stanley sat next to his mother, and I sat on the other side of Stanley. To my right, a historian made polite small talk with me while focusing most of his attention on the woman next to him. Tory and Valdorn sat across from us, not talking much.

Right after the salads were served, the table grew silent. I looked down, wondering if something was wrong with the plate. Maybe crawly things were in the lettuce? That would be bad for the Inn's reputation.

"Darling, it's been ages!" A voice like crystal rang out behind me. I looked to see who the voice belonged to and sucked in a breath. She was stunning, whoever she was; tall, with long, dark hair that cascaded past her shoulders, brilliant blue eyes, and a dress that hugged every curve. All eyes drank in her beauty. To me, she looked like an exquisite mermaid come to life.

I glanced at Stanley, who gripped his fork with a cucumber on the end. His face had turned white. His mother, however, stood and grasped the lovely creature's hands. "Sydney, dear, so good to see you! Stanley is here, of course. Although, I'm sure he told you he was coming when you saw him last weekend."

Wait, last weekend? Stanley saw *her* last weekend?

"And oh…" Birdie smiled such a warm smile that I relaxed a little bit. If she was someone Birdie liked, she must be decent. "Stanley finally brought the china we discussed. You can come over at some point for tea, and we'll examine it."

Hold on. This mermaid look-alike was the reason I'd ridden all the way to Stonington covered in dried baby puke? I decided she didn't look *that* enchanting anymore.

The mermaid directed her gaze at Stanley and gave him a tiny smirk. "Have you forgotten your manners since you've gotten into politics, dear? I know I mentioned I might not be here, but my plans changed."

Dear? She just called him dear. And now she was touching him. On the face. Like she owned him. What the heck?

I decided to be proactive about the situation. "Hi," I said. "I'm Ava." I extended my hand, which she accepted with a distinctly cold, limp grip. I thought she'd have a little grit behind her.

"Delighted to meet you. I'm Sydney," she said. "Stanley's girlfriend."

Chapter Four

Sparky ran around the apartment looking goofy with a pile of papers in his mouth. I'd gotten the puppy a couple of months ago from that lunatic Debbee before she'd tried to kill me. At least Sparky hadn't picked up any of her bad habits, but he still hadn't quite grown out of the eat-everything-in-sight stage. Giuseppe had watched the dog over the weekend, and since he insisted he didn't want any dog toys in his house, the dog had played with whatever he could find. Right now, "whatever Sparky could find" looked like important documents, judging by the legal-sized papers.

"Do you need this?" I asked, reaching down and pulling a mangled receipt from the dog's mouth. Giuseppe ran past me, hands on his head. He sort of reminded me of the dog. "What's wrong?"

"We've been throwing away all the boxes from the shipments," he said, turning in circles. "I don't have any boxes."

My brother was sweet, but sometimes he got ahead of himself. Hopefully this wasn't one of those times. "Does this mean what I think it means?"

He stopped spinning and looked at me, a wide smile plastered on his face. "We got it. They accepted our offer on the house!"

I was truly happy for him and his wife, Janine. I knew they wanted to move to a regular house with a yard for Baby Danny to play in instead of living in the apartment above Scentsations. I gave him a big hug.

"So, when's the big move?" I bent down to pet Sparky and carefully pushed more papers out of his reach. Thankfully my pocket was stuffed with tiny plastic bones filled with yummy dog treats. Sparky loved those things almost as much as he loved tennis balls. We casually exchanged papers for dog bones, and Sparky sat down and started gnawing.

"Is that all-natural? Are you giving that dog poison? What if the baby picks it up?" Giuseppe could be a bit overprotective at times.

"If you'd feed the kid regular food, he wouldn't have to scrounge around on the floor for dog bones," I said.

"I'm not going to cave to the pressure of the big business food industry. They care more about their bottom line than—"

"Listen, G, I need to ask you something," I said, knowing I had to derail this train of thought before I ended up listening to a two-hour lecture on the evils of food companies.

"Please don't call me that," he said.

"Sure," I said, not meaning it. Sparky rolled around on the floor with his treat, and I pet his silky ears. Baby Danny toddled into the room, looking delighted to see the dog. Sparky, however, got a wary look on his little puppy face. *I bet I know why.*

"How'd it go with the dog this weekend?" I asked, moving to sit on the couch.

"Fine," Giuseppe answered. "He ate the food you left, and he played a lot but didn't bark and did just fine with his bath—"

"You gave him a bath?"

Giuseppe had the grace to look a little sheepish. "We kind of had to."

I shook my head. I didn't want the details. I needed to start sneaking that child some regular food so he'd stop regurgitating all over everyone.

Dog included.

I hadn't told my brother what had happened over the weekend, mostly because I didn't feel like answering any questions. But I did want to know what was going on with Valdorn. I pondered over his comments right after the staff served the crème brûlée.

"It's nice that we're going to be spending quality time together as a family," Valdorn had said.

I tried to look anywhere but at him. Dinner had turned into one of the circles of hell and was getting worse, at least for me. And now this. The man apparently never learned the rule about swallowing your food before talking; he made me queasy every time he opened his mouth. Plus, was he talking to me? I wasn't his family.

Tory nudged him. "She's not sure if you're talking to her."

"I'm talking to her. She and I are the same, aren't we?" he said. His eyes had a faraway look that spoke of a little something extra he might've imbibed during his trip to the men's room.

It seemed I'd have to talk to him since Stanley wasn't helping me out with this one. He had angled his body slightly away from me and spoke in hushed tones with his mother. I wasn't sure Stanley would help me out with anything ever again. "How are we the same?" As soon as the words left my mouth, I regretted them. I didn't want to hear his half-baked theories on existence and spirit and whatever else he might spout.

"We're both the significant others," he said.

He was right about that, and I was grateful he recognized who I was. But it ended there.

"And we both like Giuseppe."

Wait, what? He couldn't possibly be talking about my brother. I just couldn't… actually, yes, I could. "How do you know Giuseppe?" I asked, keeping my eyes averted from his mouth. *Focus on his forehead.*

"We've met on several occasions over the years," he said. "And I'm thrilled he's hosting the shamanic workshop next weekend."

A prickling sensation started at the back of my neck. "Next weekend?"

"Yes," Valdorn said. "When Chase goes to Brewster Square to visit Stanley, I'll be with him. We'll both be in your town. Won't that be great?"

Sparky jumped on the couch next to me, interrupting my rumination. "Get that thing off my furniture," Giuseppe yelled.

I handed my brother the soggy papers I'd tossed on the end table. "When do you plan to be packed and out of here?"

Giuseppe smiled. He looked truly happy, which was good. "We close in a week and a half. It's our dream house, you know. So, despite what the home inspector said, we're moving forward with this deal."

I frowned. "Did you talk to dad about this?" Even though I had never gone through buying a house, ignoring the home inspector didn't sound like a good idea. I knew my father would try to help them as much as possible and offer his advice on repairs, but whether Giuseppe listened to him was debatable.

He waved a hand in the air. "Sure, I told him when we were moving. How was your weekend? Did you like Stanley's family? Did they approve of you?"

"The weekend was fine. I liked his family, and I think they liked me." I left out the part about Stanley introducing me as his friend, and I didn't mention Sydney. I didn't want to talk about her. Instead, I worked my way to the question that had been dancing in my mind the entire ride home. "I had dinner with someone this weekend. Some guy named Valdorn. Do you know him?"

Giuseppe crossed his eyes and screwed up his face, which was his way of saying *eeeewwwww*. His gesture relieved me. My reaction to Valdorn was based on my experiences from earlier in the year, but if my brother didn't like him, it validated my instincts. Especially because my brother liked everyone. Almost.

"I don't know him very well, but I've heard some things about him that make me wonder if he's a poser or not," he said. A poser. That was rich, coming from my brother. "I mentioned to him about the shaman coming next weekend, though. We're all excited about that."

Who wouldn't be? I kept my inner snark to myself. "He brought up the workshop," I said. "But let's talk about the more important thing: your new house. What did the home inspector say?"

Giuseppe shook his head. "Don't worry about that."

I stood and leveled a look at him. He wasn't going to brush me off. "How bad was it?"

"Listen, just because you watch those home improvement shows doesn't make you an expert in anything."

Oh boy, this cannot be good. "If there are problems, you should be careful. Ask for repairs or get a second opinion. You don't want to get stuck having to replace a foundation or fix a water problem or deal with pests—"

"I deal with pests all the time," he said, laughing. "Don't worry. I'll forward the email to you that the guy sent us after he checked out the house. It's not too bad. And we got them to lower the price because of it."

That didn't make sense to me. "But didn't you already put an offer on it?"

Giuseppe smiled. "No, we told them we wanted to put an offer on the house but insisted on the inspection first."

"They let you do that?" I was stunned.

The sellers either had a lousy agent or were desperate. My bet was on the latter, which meant whatever was wrong with this pile of lumber must be worse than I first thought.

"It's been on the market for a while, just sitting empty," he added, sensing my doubt. "They'll do anything to unload it."

I didn't know what to say to him. It might be a good deal for them, who knew. The truth was that the house my brother and his wife wanted to buy was older, with lots of charm, grace, and square footage.

And, like the last house he had insisted was fine, the one that ended up with a dead body, this one looked haunted, too. Knowing I had to spend time in this place scared the heck out of me.

Chapter Five

I gathered Sparky's belongings and almost made it out the door before Giuseppe called after me.

"I need one little thing from you," he said. My heart dropped into my stomach. Those words always got me into trouble, no matter how good his intentions were. He hadn't asked for anything after the whole almost-getting-killed-thing with Ethel, and I was getting used to my new reality. I'd enjoyed the quiet of the past two months.

"I've got a lot to do right now," I said.

"No, this is for next weekend. I need you to watch the store for me on Saturday night. I've got a ghost hunt scheduled." Relief washed through me. I could do that. I hadn't participated in a ghost hunt since my brother's last fiasco. Finding dead bodies wasn't high on my list of fun. But watching the store wasn't a problem.

"Sure, I can do that. We close at six, right?"

Giuseppe smiled. "Good. We'll be open late that night. The shaman is coming, so you'll check in people for the workshop and get all the refreshments ready. I'll pay you extra. I know you still want to take that trip to Ireland."

I'd been saving what I could for my dream trip, and this sounded like an ideal way to add to that account. "What kind of workshop is he giving?"

My brother looked at me as if I'd lost an ear. "He's teaching about shamanic journeys. Participants are instructed on the best methods for moving between worlds."

Of course. What else would a shaman talk about? Still better than the ghost-hunting thing, so I left before he found a way to pull me into that, too. Besides, it was Sunday night, and I needed to do some online research.

As Sparky and I walked down the sidewalk to our house, my cell phone started jingling from somewhere in the depths of my bag. I dug around, pushing aside dog toys and Milk-Bones to get to the phone. Finally, I pulled it out. The caller ID said it was my friend Charlie.

"Are you home yet?" she asked. "Ohmygod, I need for you to be home. Tell me you're home." My friend was generally sophisticated, poised, and charming. When she acted like this, something big happened. Or something big to her, at least.

"What's going on?"

"You have to come over. Right now."

Images of quiet time in front of the computer with Sparky at my feet faded fast. After a weekend of being on my best behavior—meaning I smiled lots and pretended to be interested in everything my hosts said—I wanted to curl up on my couch. The thing with Sydney had worn me out to the point where I didn't want to think. I wanted cake. Okay, not really cake. Just the frosting.

Charlie continued. "Come over now, and *ohgoshholycow*—" She emitted a series of high-pitched squeaks loud enough to pop Sparky's eardrums.

"Slow down. What's going on?" She might've been happy or upset; I couldn't tell. Both options sounded slightly different from the squeals coming from my phone. Maybe she needed emergency services. "Should I call 911? You sound out of breath."

"I'm fine, just… hurry!"

Charlie never asked me to drop everything for her and go to her apartment. I knew in my heart something big had happened but couldn't guess what. Sparky and I jogged to my garage on the corner behind my apartment building. We got in the car, and Sparky curled up on the front seat, looking at me with woeful eyes. "What?" I asked. "You'll be fine. We need to get to Charlie right away."

I backed out of the driveway, thinking only about whether I needed to bring something with me. Food? Wine? Oxygen? The sound of a blaring horn cut through my thoughts. I stuck my arm out the window and waved, hoping that mollified the driver behind me. I'm sure they made an equally graceful gesture back, but I didn't bother looking. Sparky kept his head down.

I made it to Charlie's house in record time, grateful that none of Brewster Square's finest were around to ticket me. Sparky and I burst through the door without knocking. Slightly winded, I stared at the scene in front of me. Charlie stood in the center of her living room. Her boyfriend, Fred, stood next to her with his arm around her. Fred's parents beamed from the couch. Everybody held a glass of champagne.

"Did you finally do something about this girlfriend situation?" I asked, speaking directly to Fred. He grinned with a look of such happiness that I couldn't help smiling back. "Congratulations, you two." Pointing to Charlie's hand, I said, "Let me see."

She held her hand out for my inspection of the stunning ring on her finger. The stone wasn't at all what I expected. I figured Fred would lavish her with something sizable. He did, after all, have a family reputation. I squinted, trying to determine whether I was looking at a diamond ring or a keyring on her finger.

"Did you pick that out, or did he surprise you?" I said, trying for tact and hoping there wasn't some weird meaning behind it. Really trying. I hugged my best friend. I knew how happy she was, and they belonged together.

Charlie laughed. "I'll get something else for an anniversary. This ring belonged to Fred's great-grandmother. It's a family heirloom."

I shot a glance at Win, who sat on the couch looking as innocent as could be. "Great-grandmother on whose side, exactly?" I asked. The sad truth was that everyone knew Win never wanted Fred to date Charlie. Charlie wasn't good enough for his son because she didn't travel in the same social circles. Not that long ago, he'd tried to break them up, and it almost worked. Almost.

"On my wife's side," Win said and smiled at me. Win never smiled at me. He stood and walked back toward the kitchen, calling over his shoulder, "Ava, I'm going to get you some champagne. You'll join us in the celebration, I hope."

Strange. Maybe Win had been taken over by some super nice aliens. "I'd love some," I said. Might as well go with it while it lasted. Who knew when the mean and nasty Win Thurgood would return.

He brought back a champagne flute for me and raised his glass. "I know we've already done this, but now that Ava's here, let's have another toast. Here's to the happy couple." Everyone raised their glasses again, and I downed half my drink in one swallow. The new Win was going to take some getting used to. I expected him to start laughing an evil *bwahaha* at any moment.

Charlie hopped around the room, more animated than I'd seen her in a while. She glowed. "I can't wait for my parents to get back from their cruise," she said. "They're going to be thrilled." While she sat with Fred and his mother discussing wedding plans, Win sidled over to me. *Uh oh, here comes Darth Win. Wonder what he's going to try to get away with saying now.* I looked everywhere but directly at the man.

"Charlie tells me you spent the weekend up in Stonington. How is Stanley these days?"

I nodded. "He's fine." It made sense that Win knew Stanley; everybody who lived in Brewster Square knew Stanley. He was the town's mayor and ran unopposed in the last election. I wondered how many people knew about Sydney. The Sydney I hadn't known existed until recently. The Sydney who had me steaming mad. But now wasn't the time for mad. Now was the time for celebrating with my friend. "Stonington's pretty," I added. A void of silence had opened up while I stewed about my life.

"And I gather you stayed with Chase and Birdie."

I narrowed my eyes. I was right. Win was up to something. Why else would he ask these questions, trying to act innocent?

"Yes. Do you know them?" I knew he did, based on what Chase said, but I wanted to hear what Win had to say.

He sipped his drink. "We all belonged to the same yacht club when we were children."

That explained the connection. But Chase had already told me he knew lots of people here. Win shook the ice in his glass, probably trying to figure out how to politely tell me I couldn't be part of Charlie's inner social circle anymore. I waited, confident there was more.

"I don't want to interfere, but you're Charlie's best friend," he said. That only meant he wanted to interfere. "She cares a great deal about you. By default, you're almost part of our family as well."

I held back a snort of disbelief. The day I became part of the Thurgood family would be the day fairies took over the world.

"Because of that, I feel it necessary to be frank," he continued. "Stanley is a wonderful person, and I admire his political achievements. He brings some much-needed energy to Brewster Square. But please be careful around Chase."

"Why?"

"That man is not to be trusted. Not at all."

CHAPTER SIX

Scentsations occupied a spot in the center of town, a couple of buildings away from where I lived—129 steps, to be exact. Unless I changed my pace and walked with shorter or longer steps. But I tried not to do that. I liked predictability; I liked knowing the distance between two points.

The downtown portion of Brewster Square surrounded the town green and included two churches, The Lilac Inn, a coffee shop, the town hall, Scentsations, and several two-story brick homes divided into apartments. My aunts and I lived in one of those homes, with me on the top floor and the aunts taking up the other two floors. I always walked to work. With my driving skills being what they were, that was best.

When I turned onto the sidewalk Monday morning, I noticed a large figure pacing in front of my brother's store. I knew right away it wasn't a customer anxious to get their vial of sandalwood essential oil.

"Been waiting for you," he said as I approached.

He couldn't have been waiting long since he knew when we opened. "Yeah, it takes me a while to walk over here." My sarcasm was in full force this morning. I took out my keys and unlocked the door. "Did you scare the crowds away? I'm not going to have any customers if you keep standing there with your official cop look."

Oliver's expression did not change. "C'mon in," I said. "I'll get a pot of coffee started, and you can tell me all about whether your aura responds better to lavender or orange blossom."

He followed me into the store. "I don't have any idea what you're talking about," he said. "But probably orange blossom. Orange is more my thing than purple."

I went behind the counter and put my purse in a drawer, then proceeded to turn on the lights and get the place ready for business. "I'll remember to get you the orange blossom essential oils for Christmas. What brings you out at this early hour?"

He made a face and looked at his watch. "It's almost nine a.m. I've been up for a while." I waited. He'd eventually tell me why he'd been pacing in front of the place. "I was wondering about your weekend. Tell me about it."

Odd. Although our friendship had progressed, his manner of asking was a bit short. Maybe he heard about Sydney and wanted to check in with me. Too bad, though, because I wasn't going to talk about it. The whole thing humiliated me. "It was something. Glad to be home." I waited. He'd want more details.

"How was Stanley's family? Were they nice? Did you spend lots of time with them, or were other people around?"

"Sounds like someone here had a rather boring weekend," I said. "Why are you so interested in what I did?" I poured water into the coffee maker, stopped, and looked at him. Something was up. I hoped he wasn't going to try to talk about Stanley. I hadn't even mentioned it to Charlie yet. Time to cut off his line of questioning. "I should set you up with someone. Sounds like you need something in your life to keep you occupied."

"What?"

"What's your type?" I asked.

"My type?" He shook his head. "Oh, no, I don't have a type. At least not a type I want you to start messing with. No. I mean, thank you, but—" He stopped, frozen by the sound of the bell on the door ringing.

I looked over, and my breath caught in my throat.

"Hello, Stanley."

"Ava, I need to talk to you. Do you have a moment?"

He'd been silent the entire ride home from Stonington, so I felt disinclined to acquiesce to his request. "I'm working right now."

He glanced at Oliver and back at me. "Listen, I know you're upset, but you wouldn't speak to me in the car."

"Excuse you, but it wasn't my job to initiate the conversation. That should've happened Saturday night. At the restaurant. Or at least, after dinner." I wasn't going to let him get away with turning his bad behavior around on me. "And frankly, I'm busy. We can talk later, at a more convenient time." I left out the unspoken part: if he didn't like it, we didn't have to talk. Ever.

With a final look at Oliver, he nodded. "Call me when you're ready." Then he was gone.

I turned back to Oliver, hoping he wouldn't ask. His phone dinged with an incoming text. When he read the screen, his lovely swarthy complexion turned almost pale. I didn't know if it was from the text or if he was coming down with something. "Everything alright?"

He shoved his phone back in his pocket. "You never answered my question."

"Which one? You bombarded me with several. Yes, I had a good enough time. Yes, I was with his family. They were nice. We had dinner. I'm not going to talk about anything that happened. Nothing extraordinary."

"What about that other guy, the one you mentioned when you called. Did he bother you?"

He was worried about me, which was sweet. Or he was hiding something, just like Stanley? No, Oliver wouldn't do that. "Valdorn? Other than his horrible table manners, no, he didn't bother me. But now that you're here, I wanted to ask you something." I'd planned on talking to him for a while, and I'd even rehearsed how I'd broach the topic. I didn't know why Oliver's opinion mattered to me, but it did. Maybe I valued his friendship more than I realized.

"Did something happen this weekend that's got you on edge? You seem nervous," he said.

"No, this has nothing to do with the weekend. This is about my career, or what I want as a career." I couldn't work for my brother forever, or forever would be very short for both of us. I needed something more than retail work.

Oliver looked dubious. "Talk to someone who does career counseling or something like that."

I ignored him. "I'm considering becoming a private investigator." I held up a hand to stop the protest I knew was coming. "Listen, it makes sense to me, but I wanted to talk it through with someone in law enforcement."

He sighed. "What about this makes sense to you?"

Emboldened, I continued. "I know it's going to be mostly boring, checking on cheating husbands, surveillance, stuff like that."

Oliver walked around the store as if he couldn't contain his energy. It was hard to tell if he was upset, anxious, or restless. "I can't tell you what to do, but I don't think that particular career would be a good choice. There're a lot of unknowns with investigations, even when you think everything's cut and dry."

"But isn't the unknown sort of my specialty?"

Oliver had a hint of a smile. "Yes and no. The problem is when the unknown blows up in your face. You might start a case thinking all you have to do is get pictures of the cheater, right?" I nodded to show I was following, so he continued. "You're sitting in your car waiting for some cheating schmuck, and the next thing you know, the guy shows up with a baseball bat and comes after you. Can you defend yourself from a perp who wants to kill you?"

This had more to do with Oliver's innate distrust of humans in general than anything that might happen. But I needed to humor him. "You're right; I'm going to have to plan for that eventuality," I said.

"Don't humor me," he said. "Why are you so hell-bent on doing this?"

I didn't have to think about it since I'd already given it lots of thought. "I want to make a difference in the world. I want to know I did something that mattered to someone. After helping find Ethel's killer, I felt like I'd been part of something that helped people."

Oliver looked up at the ceiling. "You want to help people? Get a job as a social worker."

I was stunned. He hadn't heard a word I'd said. I opened my mouth to tell him so, but his cell phone interrupted me. He glanced at me and said, "Seriously. I don't want you to get hurt." He pulled the phone out, looked at it, and walked to the other side of the store. I tried to look busy, but I was still able to eavesdrop. After that nasty comment, I didn't care if it was ethical or not. He didn't have to be so mean, even if it was because he only wanted to keep me safe.

I listened in on his end of the conversation. "Yeah, I know… No, probably not… I can't say. You're kidding, right?" I was frustrated with these bits and pieces of a one-sided phone call but couldn't ask him to use his speaker phone. I almost wished I had when he said, "Even if I did care about you, this wouldn't work. Not now and not ever, especially after Jennie."

Chapter Seven

Sparky had a way of making me feel better about life. There's nothing like a dog to give you a good perspective on what's important and what's not. As he bounced down the street next to me, pulling on his leash now and then, I couldn't help but marvel at his sheer joy. Whenever he saw someone, no matter who it was, his butt started wagging. It didn't even matter to him that it was seven o'clock in the morning; he was ready to go. On the other hand, I needed three cups of coffee just to find the door.

It was now two days after we'd returned from Stonington. I'd relented and invited Stanley to join Sparky and me on our morning walk. He had called me after work last night, too, and I just needed clarity on what happened.

He walked with us, holding my hand as we made our way across the Green and down Elm Street. I didn't pull away, but I was confused. The silence between us gave me some space to organize my thoughts. I didn't get a chance to talk to Oliver after his phone call. He said he'd catch up with me later and left. Dealing with customers, and later my brother, pushed all thoughts of Oliver aside, but the memory resurfaced as we strolled through the downtown.

Who had Oliver been talking to? I couldn't exactly ask him about it, as it wasn't polite to listen to other people's conversations. He'd been kind to me during my recovery after Ethel's murder, so it wouldn't hurt to show some concern for his life. He'd think I was nosy—which I was—but I did care about him as a friend. We'd come a long way from our initial animosity toward each other.

I thought more about how he reacted to my private investigator question. He must've responded negatively out of concern for my safety. Not that his answer was a good one, but at least I understood where he was coming from.

Oliver was in a relationship. But with whom? Someone serious. He wouldn't tell someone he cared about them if he didn't mean it. That wasn't his style. But wait—he hadn't said anything about love. He'd said, "even if I cared about you" or something like that. What did he mean? Did he even like this person?

A Mexican drug lord kidnapped his wife, Jennie, in Arizona—a story he loathed to talk about. I searched my memory and tried to dredge up stories about his wife. The police and other various agencies involved had never found her. Would that mean he was widowed now or simply in marriage-limbo?

We'd been walking awhile, and Stanley and I still weren't talking. He should be the one to start talking, apologizing, groveling, any of the above. The silence stretched to an uncomfortable length. I cleared my throat and pulled my hand away. Nothing. Stanley walked with his head down, oblivious to his surroundings.

I said the first thing that came to my mind to prod him out of his world. I pointed to the sky. "Is that a hawk?" I wouldn't know the difference between a hawk and a bluebird, but I had to try something.

"Mmmph," Stanley said.

Why wouldn't he explain mermaid-Sydney to me? Was she his girlfriend?

I'd known Stanley for years, but I'd never seen him with her. That didn't mean anything, though. He could've been meeting her in different places or avoiding me when she was around. His parents seemed comfortable with her. He must've changed his mind about us.

I stopped in my tracks. Sparky hopped around me, tangling his leash in my legs. The only way to know was to ask. "Did I do something wrong?"

Stanley looked up. His face was a mask of confusion. "No, not that I know of. Why?"

"Because you're not talking to me. You're not even looking at what's around you. You didn't talk in the car all the way home. All you said was 'ignore Sydney,' which is a tough thing to do." I was getting mad all over again and getting mad wouldn't produce answers; it'd only produce me yelling at Stanley. I took a breath and gained control over my emotions. "Look at you. You're staring at the ground. I need to know what's going on. Why did that person say she was your girlfriend? Are you seeing her? We're supposed to be honest with each other."

It was more difficult to say aloud than I thought it would. I thought Stanley was one of the good guys, but I'd been wrong before.

He bent to untangle Sparky, and I let go of the leash. He stood and handed it back to me. "She's not quite my girlfriend. But she used to be. We still talk." He broke eye contact. "I'm sorry, this is hard for me."

I held tight to my barely-there composure. "Oh, that's too bad. It's been easy for me."

He squinted. "What?"

"Yeah, that was sarcasm. How the hell do you think I feel?"

"I know—I'm sorry. Here's the thing." We reached a bench, sat down, and faced each other. "Sydney and I dated for a long time. I thought we were gonna get married. Our families were friends, and we grew up knowing each other. But one day I..." he trailed off.

He wasn't going to tell me the whole story. I had a feeling he was about to get up and leave. "Just say it. You'll feel better after you say it," I said. I needed to hear it, the whole thing.

"You're right." Squaring his shoulders, he continued. "One day, I saw her with another man. I saw her kissing my friend, Jack. It was clear they were lovers. That was the day I left. And I never went back."

It partly made sense, but a lot of information was missing. "You saw her with another guy, a friend of yours, and you didn't confront her?"

He shook his head. "No. I drove away. That was it."

"You left her?"

"No, I left town. I moved here, to Brewster Square."

"Let me get this straight. You never once yelled at her. You never talked to this Jack person or asked them what the hell they were doing or confronted her or your friend about their behavior?" Stanley shook his head. "And you never once called to ask for your DVDs back or anything?"

Stanley thought about it. "I spoke to her, yeah, but she didn't have any DVDs of mine."

Exasperation clutched at my chest. "Stanley, that's not the point. The point is everybody leaves something behind in a relationship. If we stopped seeing each other right this minute, wouldn't you want your Ursula K. Le Guin book back?"

"I have an Ursula K. Le Guin book?"

I bit back a bitter laugh. "Yes. It's sitting in my living room. And I'm sure you left stuff behind at her house, too. All this time you ignored what happened with her and your friend. Did you ignore your friend, too? Jack? What did you tell your family?"

Stanley shrugged. "Yes. And nothing."

A moment ticked by while I waited for more. I'd be waiting a long time since he just slumped there on the bench. I prodded him along. "What did Jack do? Did he know you saw them?"

"Sydney told him. She liked playing those types of games. He called me a few times, but I told him to forget it. I forgave him, but I didn't want to hang out with him again."

I understood his feelings about his friend, but why did he still talk to Sydney? Maybe because his mother liked her. "Did your mother ask about her?"

"I always changed the subject."

The whole family had a habit of hiding from the truth. Win's warning about Chase flitted through my head, but I didn't have time to think about it. Things were bad enough without Mr. Pompous making my life harder. Honestly, this was so far from anything I had ever expected of Stanley. I didn't know what to do with him now. It occurred to me his whole family thought I was merely Stanley's friend. Another thought occurred to me. "Stanley, did your mother invite her to that dinner?"

His eyes widened. "No, she wouldn't… I mean, why? She couldn't know…"

"You're an idiot." I stood to walk away. Sparky jumped up to follow.

"Wait!" He jumped up, grabbed my arm, and took a step closer to me. "I know how this looks. Right now, everything is a big mess. Not just this thing with Sydney, but everything."

He sounded miserable, and I felt bad for him despite my anger. "Is something going on with your job as mayor?" As the mayor of Brewster Square, Stanley dealt with all types of people and their problems. He never talked about it. Then again, I never asked.

"No," he said. I waited. He was going to have to talk sooner or later. After a few moments, he finally added, "I don't know." Clearly, there was more.

"Stanley, are you done with this relationship?"

There, I said it. It was out in the open, and no matter how he answered, I could start to move forward.

Chapter Eight

No," he said. "Not at all. I love being with you."

I'd have to think about what that meant, if it meant anything. "Start talking. I don't have all day."

A sad smile crept onto his face. "You're right. I'm sorry." He pointed toward a small stand of trees. "Do you see that bird in the tree? The one sitting on the lower branch. He's sort of brown or gray, I can't tell. The little one."

The bird perched with his head cocked as if ready for flight. "Yes. He's just a bird. Doesn't look dangerous or anything to me."

"Do you know what kind of bird it is?"

"No." I guess I needed to study ornithology. His family sure was into birdwatching.

"Neither do I."

"Maybe it's a wren," I offered, yanking on Sparky's leash as he began to eat some grass. "Or a sparrow. Definitely not a cardinal."

Stanley shook his head. "It could be a phoenix for all I know."

"I don't think they're real."

"They're not real, but that's not the point." His face looked pained, as if he had stomach cramps. "My parents are both amazing birders, and they can tell a type of bird just by looking at a silhouette forty feet in the air or listening to the birdsong. Most of the time, I don't notice the birds in my backyard." He shifted from foot to foot. "I don't even have a bird feeder," he whispered.

Not quite the existential crisis I'd expected, but Stanley did have to find a way to deal with this. And I was going to have to ignore the fact that he was pushing the whole Sydney thing aside—again. "C'mon, let's keep walking," I said and grabbed his hand. "First of all, just because your parents do something doesn't mean you're obligated to do the same thing. Does it matter if you can tell the difference between crows and ravens?"

"It matters to my father. When I was little, he used to take us on hikes through the woods and point out all the birds and frogs and plants and stuff. I liked being in the woods, but I didn't pay much attention to the names. I had fun hiking."

I nodded. "That sounds like most kids."

"My dad expected us to know these things once he told us. If he pointed out a hawk, he'd expect us to differentiate a Cooper's hawk from a red-tailed hawk. And for a while, I tried, I did. But he'd get mad when I made a mistake, so I stopped listening to him. It got worse from there."

"You rebelled against your father trying to teach you about birds," I said. "Sounds natural to me."

"But now that I'm an adult, I have no reason to rebel. We get along great. I love my dad. He's coming for the weekend, and I know he'll want to talk about this stuff because that's the whole reason he's coming—for that lecture."

"Stop right there. Just because he's visiting doesn't mean you have to talk about birds. Besides, it doesn't matter if you know anything about birds or buffalo. What matters is spending time with your dad."

I turned around and started heading back. We both had things to do that day, and I needed time alone to process what to do about Sydney. Was I prepared to call it quits because some woman claimed to be his girlfriend? If anything, I was ready to end the relationship because he didn't put her in her place and stand up for what we had. Have.

"Do you know all the building codes for Brewster Square?" I asked.

He shrugged.

"But you still have meetings with the building inspectors. Can you do an assessment for real estate here in town? Are you able to figure out how to reroute the drainage systems in the event of a flood catastrophe?"

"I don't think the drainage systems can be rerouted," he said. "What are you getting at?"

"Whatever, that's not the point." Even though he was super-smart about computers, he sure could be dense about things. "The point is, you don't have to know about a subject to discuss it with others. You're a reasonably intelligent man. You'll find a way to talk to your dad this weekend. Relax and enjoy your time together, that's all."

He leaned down and kissed me lightly on the lips. "Thank you." When he straightened, I caught a shadowy movement to the side of us. Something— or someone—stepped behind a tree in the yard across the street.

That's weird. Usually people don't walk around ducking behind trees like cartoon characters.

Stanley hadn't noticed. "The only other thing that I've got to worry about is my sister," he said.

Law enforcement always posted things like: *If you see something, say something.* I should say something. "Did you...?"

"Did I what?"

"I thought I saw someone. Across the street."

Stanley turned and scanned the area behind him. "People are out in their yards. It's not that early." Sparky yanked against his leash, so we continued. "What did you think of Valdorn?"

I wished I knew what Stanley thought of him before opening my big mouth. But, whatever. Honesty and all that. "I don't know," I said. "Something about him doesn't seem quite—"

"Right," Stanley finished. "And it's just like my sister to go and hook up with another loser. It's not the first time she's brought home a chooch."

"A what?"

"You know, a moron. Completely wrong for her."

I laughed. "That's what I thought you said. I haven't heard that word since I was in the fifth grade."

"I don't think she can help herself. A human disaster shows the slightest bit of interest in her, and she starts dating him. Why can't she look at my parents and see what a good relationship is supposed to be?"

I clamped my mouth shut. I wasn't getting involved in family dynamics. Not at this point, anyway. Especially since I wasn't sure of our future together. Win's words snaked through my mind again: *That man is not to be trusted. Not at all.* But how well did Win know Chase? Did Charlie know what her future father-in-law thought of Stanley's father? Hopefully she did so we could talk about it without me explaining the whole situation.

"Anyway, I'm going to have my dad and *the boyfriend* staying with me this weekend, so I'd better get over it."

"How about I come over on Friday and help you cook dinner? We can have a relaxing night in, no stress." His answer would help me figure out where he stood with our relationship. If he didn't want me there Friday, it probably meant the perfect Sydney would be there. And here I was, willing to be in the same room as the weirdo boyfriend, Valdorn. That alone should've clued him into the fact that I was on his side.

"Perfect! They'll be at the house after the Yale lecture, around five-ish. I'll be home all day, so you can come over anytime."

It's time. Time to tell him. You know he cares about you, so don't worry.

"So, I wanted to talk to you about something I've been considering."

"Shoot. I'm listening."

"It all started with Ethel's murder."

"I hated your involvement with that. It's a wonder you didn't get killed."

"It wasn't that bad."

"Stop downplaying the situation. That guy came at you with a knife. And that woman, the one who caused all the insanity, you're lucky she didn't kill you, too."

"But it all worked out." My breath came in short gasps. Who did he think he was, talking to me like that? What happened to the nonconfrontational boyfriend who couldn't even speak to his cheating girlfriend?

"Only because your guardian angels were working overtime. Do me a favor, don't ever do that again."

"I'll try not to—"

"I didn't ask you to try; I asked you to stay out of danger."

"I don't know if that's going to be possible."

"Why not?"

"Because I'm thinking about becoming a private investigator."

Chapter Nine

The smell of bacon permeated the air. Bacon-wrapped scallops and bacon-wrapped shrimp. Other good things sizzled in front of me, too: London broil with horseradish, puff pastry filled with Seafood Newburg, and sliced baked apples spread in front of warm brie with syrup-drizzled toasted pecans. A variety of vine-ripened tomatoes sat on a plate, filled with an explosion of flavor. Sliced tomatoes topped with basil and fresh mozzarella were artfully arranged on a gleaming white platter. No dried chicken and stringy asparagus for my friend Charlie. And her soon-to-be in-laws wouldn't tolerate plebian food, either, especially at the grand occasion of their only son's wedding.

We were seated in the tasting room of one of New Haven's most sought-after venues for weddings, Chez Chez. It struck me as a ridiculous name, but what did I know about naming a restaurant? Charlie told me it was one of the places they were considering for their wedding reception, and she wasn't sure she liked it. First, the name. Blech. Second, she wanted something more down-to-earth, maybe even on the beach. But she wasn't averse to free food, which was what we were getting in the hopes that we (meaning Charlie) would book the place for the wedding of the century.

And the food kept coming. The wedding planner, a small, nervous woman with black, square glasses, flitted about from one dish to the next. The dizzying array of choices in front of us caused some difficulty in keeping track of what we'd eaten. Fortunately, the wedding planner wrote everything down on her trusty clipboard. Everything. Probably even things having nothing to do with food. I'm pretty sure she wrote down some mean things about me since I kept distracting the bride-to-be with conversations about non-wedding things.

"He said he didn't mind?" Charlie asked. "Even after that whole lecture about you almost getting killed?"

"He said that if that's what I wanted to do, he supported my decision. Then he asked if I had to work this weekend as if I hadn't said anything important. I was pretty mad. Maybe he picked up on it."

"Guilt," Charlie declared. "He's ashamed of the whole Sydney thing, and he's trying to figure out how to be a good boyfriend. He went from 'I'm going to make sure you're safe' Neanderthal man to 'Oh if that's what you want, it's fine by me' in like one second. Trust me, I know guilt when I hear it."

"Something else happened, though, that you should know about," I said. "It's a little odd, but I'm trying not to worry. Stanley and I saw—"

"Ma'am, are you interested in trying some pinot noir?" The wedding planner lady interrupted, offering me a half-full glass of wine.

"Sure." She might've been trying to get me drunk so I'd shut up, but I wasn't about to turn down alcohol, especially since I needed to tell Charlie who was lurking around the park when Stanley and I had our conversation. Luckily, I didn't have to drive because Fred was coming to pick us up.

"Ladies, we need to stay focused. Even though the bride has not yet picked a date, we need to be ready with our choices. Planning an event of this magnitude is no easy feat."

I exchanged a look with Charlie. An event of this magnitude? How big was this going to be? Knowing Fred's family, it'd be *the* wedding of the season. And knowing Charlie, also exquisite.

"So, without having a date, we can still begin our preparations." Wedding-planner lady continued. "With a date—"

"You'll know when we decide," Charlie interrupted. Turning to me, she asked, "Do you have to work tonight?"

"Yes. But that means I get to skip the stupid ghost hunt because G scheduled some workshop thing at the store that I'm overseeing. Also, Stanley's dad and some guy are coming to town for the weekend."

"He hates it when you call him G. And what do you mean by 'some guy'? Does Stanley's dad have a boyfriend?"

"No. Stanley's sister's boyfriend. He's a creep."

"What makes him a creep?"

"He just is."

"Okaaaay." Charlie's tone told me she was trying to understand my reasoning.

"His name is Valdorn," I added.

"A-ha." Now Charlie knew exactly what kind of guy this was. "Do you have to spend time with him?"

"God, I hope not. That would suck. He's all New Age-y and obnoxious. But I'll be spending time with Chase since he's staying at Stanley's house."

"What's his family like?" she asked around a mouthful of something else wrapped in bacon.

"Nice. Not pretentious. His sister's kind of odd, hard to get close to. But his dad was welcoming, and his mom seemed to warm up to me. They're an average family, a little better off than most. Comfortable."

"You don't want rich like Fred's family. Rich is weird. Everything about them is weird. I think something happened to them, like they got hit on the head by a meteor, or they've been replaced by pod people."

"What are you talking about?" Charlie didn't have the best relationship with her soon-to-be father-in-law, but she'd always been close to her soon-to-be mother-in-law.

"Win's been different. If I didn't know any better, I'd think he caught some serious illness or something." She leaned in closer, her voice dropping to a harsh whisper. Wedding-planner lady wasn't listening, but if she was, at least now she'd have to move closer to get the inside scoop. "He told me he was glad Fred and I worked things out, and he hoped we wouldn't wait too long to start a family." She dabbed a napkin at the corner of her mouth before tossing back the remains of her pinot noir. "Clearly he has some awful disease because under normal circumstances, he'd never say a thing like that."

CHAPTER TEN

Charlie wasn't the dramatic type, but now that the wedding was happening, all her fears must've bubbled to the surface.

"I don't think he's sick," I said.

"Then what happened? Did three ghosts visit him? Did he hit his head on the marble countertop in their kitchen?"

"Things happened in his life that made him see the world a bit differently." Charlie must've forgotten the information we learned about Win not so long ago. She did have more pressing matters on her mind, what with planning the wedding of the century and all. "Remember Ethel?"

Charlie paused, her fork full of bacon-wrapped duck halfway to her mouth. Her brow wrinkled. "They were a thing."

I nodded. "Most definitely a thing. A big-deal, love-of-your-life thing."

"You think her death changed Win?"

"All deaths change us. I'd like to think that Win reevaluated his life when Ethel died."

"Enough to start being nice to me?"

I hesitated. She had a point. Win had gone out of his way to expel Charlie from his son's world and insert someone he thought was proper.

"Isn't that what happened with him and Ethel? Didn't his family decide she wasn't the right sort of person for him?"

Understanding dawned. "He's trying to make something right. That's…" she struggled for words. "I don't know what that is. Either it's delightful that he's come to his senses, or it's scary that he's trying to relive his life through us."

"Don't look a gift horse in the mouth."

"How does that saying apply to me?"

I shrugged. "He's being nice to you. That's a gift, right?"

"What are we going to do about the cake?" Wedding-planner lady stood with her hands on her hips, staring at Charlie and me as if we'd skipped our high school algebra class. "It won't get made if we don't have decisions. People will talk about this event for quite some time, you know. We mustn't disappoint."

"Mmm," Charlie said. "You know what? I read something in a magazine somewhere that said the latest thing for weddings was a new kind of cake. Very trendy." She sat back and raised an eyebrow, a sure sign the wedding planner was in trouble.

"Unique and trendy are good. But we must be sure to—"

"I know, right?" Charlie plowed on, this time with a smile pasted on her face. I got comfortable, wishing I had popcorn.

"Are you talking about the one made with the candy bars?" I asked, trying to be helpful. That's what friends are for, right?

Charlie smiled at me. "I considered that one."

"Oh, no, we mustn't limit ourselves—"

"But I saw one even better." Charlie crossed her arms over her chest. Out of the corner of my eye, I saw something—or someone—cupping their hands around their face and peering through the front window. We were far enough back and hidden by the dim lighting, so maybe she couldn't see us. I shrank down in my seat, just in case. Charlie would have a conniption once she knew who was out there.

"We must remember that the sharing of the cake is a glorious symbol of good fortune for your future as well as—"

"Charlie," I interrupted, staring at the front window, "we need to—"

"Exactly." Wedding-planner lady continued as if I were on her side. "Not only will this event begin your lives…" I stopped listening to her drone, riveted instead by the person in the window who was now frantically waving at me.

Rats. She saw me.

"Twinkie cake," Charlie said. "I want a Twinkie cake for my wedding."

"You can't—"

Something had to be done before she came through the front door. I wasn't ready for this. "I think we need to—"

"Yes, we need to take our time evaluating our choices."

"Yep, choices. Can we talk about this later?" Charlie gave me a look, clearly disappointed that I wasn't having as much fun as she was at creating angst for the wedding planner.

"What's wrong with a Twinkie cake?" Charlie kept it up, getting what she could out of it. Since the wedding planner bugged me, I understood, but we were about to have other problems.

"We need more wine before we make a decision," I said, reverting to *we*, like the wedding planner. It was all I had at that point.

"Indeed," wedding planner said, clapping her hands together. *Who does that?* She hurried off to the bar to get more alcohol.

"What's going on with you?" Charlie asked. "That could have been fun."

"Yes, but right now, we have a situation."

Two wine glasses appeared before us. "Moscato."

Charlie looked up at wedding planner lady, who was nervously fidgeting with her hair and glasses. "I hate the sweet wines. Can we try a chardonnay, dry?"

I'll give her credit for not even hesitating before scooping the glasses up and scurrying back to the bar. It probably didn't matter to her, anyway, since she was going to drink those two drinks herself. At least I would have if I were her and had to deal with future brides all day long.

"What situation?"

I hesitated. I was still mad about what had happened, but it wasn't going to go away. "I've been getting letters. So far I've gotten three or four."

"Letters?" Charlie asked, incredulity lacing her voice. "Like actual written on paper sent through the postal service letters?"

"I know, odd, but that's what you do when you don't have access to a computer and have to write to someone from a mental health facility."

There was a moment of silence while Charlie stared at me in horror. "No."

"Yes. Debbee." Debbee, who had tried to kill me not so long ago. Not just me, but the whole town. In her defense, she didn't realize she was poisoning the people of Brewster Square. True, I had the love of my life, Sparky, because of Debbee, but I also had nightmares and a bad reaction to people like Valdorn. Last I knew, she'd been sent to a facility, a fancy place with standing reservations for the showbiz elite.

"From that place in New Canaan?" she asked. I nodded, and she shook her head in disbelief. "Who knew she came from such a prominent family? And why the heck is she writing to you?" Charlie smiled at wedding-planner lady, who'd brought new wine glasses and had probably polished an entire bottle of moscato off by now. I would if I were her.

"I guess her family is the reason she was able to go to Fairfield County to 'recover' from her little episode. She's writing to me because she wants to be friends."

Charlie choked on her wine. "Friends?"

"Sit tight, dear," Wedding-planner lady said after patting Charlie on the back. "I have a surprise for you."

"She wants to put everything behind us and work together for our common good, overcoming obstacles that might be remnants from a past life, and together we can create a sustainable friendship that will benefit the entire community."

"She said that?" Charlie was horrified.

I'd gotten past being appalled and had landed on mad. "That's not all."

"There's more?" She took a big swallow of her wine, and so did I. I needed fortification for the next part. I clunked my glass back on the table as wedding-planner lady came back with a tray filled with a large assortment of small plates.

"There's more, but it's not the letters. It's her. She's here, at the front window, waving at us. Or at me," I said. "She saw me."

The door opened and Debbee waltzed in, waving at me the whole time. "I knew it was you. I knew it," she said, arriving at our table slightly out of breath. "Ooohhh," Debbee breathed, "Cake!"

Chapter Eleven

I'd had an entire day to come to grips with the fact that Ms. Crazy-pants was back in town. I couldn't do much about her being back, but I knew exactly what to do about her request to be my friend: ignore her.

I saved the letters she wrote me, despite them being both menacing and eerily casual (*Hi Ava! It's me, Debbee, and I'm better now! Sorry I tried to kill you. I didn't mean it! LOL!*). I figured I might need them for evidence at some point. Evidence of what, I wasn't sure (*Your Honor, she wants to be my friend. Isn't that some sort of crime?*). If anything happened to me, they were clues, so I resisted flushing them down the toilet or leaving them out for Sparky to chew on.

Charlie agreed with my initial concerns but quickly decided Debbee was as harmless as Sparky bouncing around Chez Chez, wanting to be friends. She proceeded to use it to her advantage.

"So, Debbee, we're trying to plan a cake for my wedding," she said while wedding-planner lady hovered. "Have you ever heard of Twinkie cake?"

"I've had one of those," Debbee said. "Apart from the fact that most of the ingredients are chemically processed, it was delish! It'd be amazing if you could get one made with organic ingredients." I almost felt bad for wedding-planner lady at that point, but the horrified look on her face made it worth a little guilt.

Charlie and I managed to sneak out while Debbee extolled the virtues of organic cake to wedding-planner lady. I had a feeling Charlie might have to find a new wedding planner.

The next day, Stanley stopped by the store to see me. When I told him about Debbee showing up at Chez Chez, he was reserved in expressing his apprehension, as if he were afraid to say the wrong thing. It turns out that was the wrong thing.

"Aren't you even a little worried?" I asked him while I put a new roll of receipt paper in the cash register. "We saw her yesterday in the park. Then she showed up at Charlie's taste testing thing. What if she's stalking me?" I finished and slammed the cover shut.

"Sure, I'm a bit worried, if you are. Are you?"

"My feelings shouldn't count toward your reaction," I said, doing my best to stare him down.

"But I don't want to crowd you."

"How is caring about my safety crowding me?"

"Remember when I cared enough about your safety to ask you to stop looking for a murderer a couple of months ago?"

"That's because you demanded I stop doing something instead of talking about how you felt. This time I'm asking you how you feel."

He shook his head and muttered something about a headache. "Are you still coming over for dinner?"

Fine, I could play this game too and ignore the entire Ava-is-at-risk conversation. "Yes, I'm coming to help. I said I would, so I will. For you, your father, and the creepy guy your sister's dating."

He picked up on something in my tone (with all that subtlety, how surprising) and put his arms around me, the first hug I'd gotten from him in days. Tears threatened, so I hugged him back and nudged him away. No crying in front of him, not now.

"What should we make for dinner?" I asked.

"I don't know. A roast? Or something like beef Wellington."

Was he kidding? Beef Wellington? "Have you bought any food yet?"

"I wasn't sure what we were going to make."

Thank goodness. "You know I can't be there until around four, right?"

He nodded. "That works."

"How about we grill some chicken? The cleanup won't be so bad. I'll tell you what to use, and you can let the meat marinate this afternoon. We'll put the vegetables on the grill. Is the boyfriend a vegetarian?" I'd spent so much time avoiding him eating at the restaurant that I hadn't noticed what he'd ordered.

Stanley wrinkled his brow. "I don't think so. I don't care if he is, anyway. I'm only having him here because he's with my dad. Otherwise, he wouldn't be staying."

Later that evening, Stanley and I sat outside with Chase and Valdorn. Dinner was a hit, and everyone ate with gusto, including me. I hadn't had lunch earlier because the store was hectic, and Giuseppe left me alone to deal with everything. G said he had mountains of paperwork to sort through. Usually when he said things like that, it was code for *I'm going to take a nap upstairs*, but this time he sat in the small office behind the counter and worked on loan documents. Customers hopefully missed the occasional potty language coming from the other room, since the store's vibe was supposed to be peace, love, and all that. Banks are known to induce that sort of language from most people, so it wasn't like anyone would blame him if they did hear him.

Once we settled after dinner with another glass of wine—my third of the night, to ease the tension a bit—I asked Chase about the lectures they had attended that day.

"It was a collaboration between researchers from various universities discussing current and future deviations in migration patterns due to climate change," Chase explained. "Most of the talks centered on the migration of butterflies, a subject I'm familiar with but in no way an expert. Still, the panels were excellent."

In the spirit of friendliness, I tried to include the mostly silent and still sort of creepy Valdorn in the conversation and asked, "Did you enjoy the lecture?"

He looked up from navel-gazing to stare at the sky. "Sure."

"Did you hear the same ones about birds?"

"Um, no, I stayed with the butterfly group."

A real talker, that one. I'd find a way to engage in polite conversation with him if only to prove I could. Stanley didn't help; he'd fallen quiet after dinner. It was up to me to keep the conversation rolling. "So which butterflies have changed their patterns the most?"

"The most what?" Valdorn asked as he sniffed and wiped his nose on his hemp sleeve.

"The most…" I thought the question had been straightforward. Better not to assume anything, especially when conversing with someone who had a name like Valdorn.

"…deviations?" I finished.

"The talk I went to focused on a study of white storks that suggested they've been overwintering in Europe," Chase said. "However, data indicates that nearly half of U.S. migratory bird species will be considered endangered during this century."

I was stunned. "Wait, what? Does that mean they'll die?"

Chase shrugged. "We don't know at this point, but it doesn't look good.

We're altering our landscape and cannot predict how the species will cope. Monarch butterflies are struggling, too, and sometimes overwintering. Valdorn, what did you think of the data?"

"It doesn't look good. Yeah. Hard to tell what's going to happen."

I narrowed my eyes at creepy boyfriend with the drippy nose. That wasn't an answer; that was parroting back what Chase said.

"Anyway, the research is important. Hopefully we'll figure out a way to slow the inevitable." Chase regarded Valdorn again. "I noticed you talking to the presenters. How do you know Prescott and Coates?"

Valdorn reentered navel-gazing mode and muttered something none of us understood.

"Prescott and Coates? That sounds like the name of a law firm," I said.

Chase laughed. "Yes, it does." He sipped his wine, a healthy swig. I guess those conferences are brutal. "These kids are Ivy Leaguers, and they know their stuff. Most impressive."

I pressed creepy guy to answer the question. "Were Prescott and Coates friends of yours?"

"No, I… well, I might've seen them around. Somewhere. Before."

Uncomfortable silence hovered around us. Finally Chase said, "You talked with them awhile."

"Yeah, we were just… you know, talking about cosmic nature stuff. They were cool." He took the elastic out of his hair and shook his ponytail out.

Cosmic nature stuff? Chase and Stanley were dubious, and I didn't blame them. Valdorn was making up everything as he went along. But the real question, the one that sent chills through my entire body, was the one I wanted to ignore: what was he hiding?

Chapter Twelve

For most retailers, Saturdays—depending on the time of year and terror threat—are busy. Giuseppe had taken care of all his banking necessities for the new house during the week, which meant he'd be available to work the floor with me. The prospect of buying a new home had my brother acting with exemplary customer service. I, on the other hand, wasn't in the mood.

My night at Stanley's had ended with Sydney calling Chase's cell phone. "Hi, Sydney!" Chase boomed, loud enough to burst her eardrum, fingers crossed. "He's right here. Hasn't he given you his new cell phone number?" Chase handed the phone to Stanley, who got up and went into the house, leaving me with his father and creepy guy. Thirty minutes later, he handed the phone back to his father and sat down as if nothing had happened.

"Everything good?" I asked.

"Yes."

Maybe Stanley didn't want to talk in front of his father. "Why don't we put the wine back in the fridge? And don't we have some dessert in the kitchen to bring out?" *I should have brought them a Twinkie cake. It could have been wedding research.*

"Don't worry about the wine; someone may want more. Dessert is for later."

I left soon after that.

On my early Saturday morning walk with Sparky, I gave him extra treats and stopped to let him pee on as many little things as he wanted. My dog was an expert territory marker. Whenever I thought he might be done peeing, he always had a little left to mark something else. And boy did he show those squirrels who was in charge.

"I can always depend on you, Sparky." His tail wagged at hearing his name, and he looked at me, hopeful I might have a dog treat in my pocket. I did. "You wouldn't leave me during dinner to go talk to a traitorous ex, would you," I said, handing him a steak-flavored treat. The look he gave me stated that he'd never leave my side if I kept the treats coming.

Dogs are much more faithful than people.

I brought him to work with me and settled him on his dog bed in the office. I'd been bringing Sparky awhile now, although my brother initially had reservations. His mind changed once he realized what a marketing pull Sparky had. People who usually never came into the store came in to see my dog. Sparky mostly stayed on his bed and slept (he reminded me a little of my brother that way) or chewed on his toys. Once in a while he'd come out to say hello, especially if a child was present. He loved kids.

Today, he was different. He followed me around the store even when I halfheartedly shooed him back to the office. My brother, always the businessperson, asked, "Can we pose Sparky over by the window?"

"No," I snapped.

He waited for a beat, then said, "How about if he—"

"I'll put him in the office, don't worry." I stomped away, calling my dog as I did so. When I came back out, Giuseppe was helping a customer.

"We have several chakra-balancing scents. I just got a new shipment. I'll be right back." Walking past me, he whispered, "You good? You seem a little… you know."

"My chakras need balancing, too," I answered, knowing sarcasm would get him to leave me alone. In case that didn't work, I added, "And it's that time of the month." Best way to get a guy to leave you alone, hands down.

He nodded sagely and kept walking, returning a moment later with his arms full of candles, crystals, and books for the customer, a well-dressed, middle-aged woman. "They sell kits for these things, but I believe it's better to personalize according to your vibrational needs," he quipped, sailing down the aisle and smiling at her.

I shook my head. I had to admit that this sort of job suited him. He knew the products and wanted to sell them to people, whereas I thought the customer who asked for chakra-balancing needed balancing of a different kind. Or maybe I was bitter.

"Perhaps you would also benefit from our wonderful workshop tonight," Giuseppe continued. "A powerful shamanic experience is set to happen after we close, in a little while. If you're interested, the flyers are next to the cash register. Class begins at seven, but people arrive early for a little meet and greet. My sister, Ava, will be hostess." All six customers turned and looked at me when Giuseppe pointed my way. I gave a weak little smile and waved. What fresh new hell was this? *At least it's not a ghost hunt.*

Giuseppe wandered toward me, acting as if he happened to be walking in my direction. "What?" I said as soon as he got close enough. Sparky slunk out of the office at the exact moment, slowly making his way over to me. I swear that dog knew when I was upset and did his best to comfort me.

Giuseppe looked like he was trying to balance a Ming dynasty vase on a toothpick. "I thought you could maybe not worry about the customers right now and focus on setting up for tonight."

I nodded. "That's a good idea. Where do you want this thing to happen?"

He pointed to the back area. "You can set up the chairs in a circle. If you need help clearing—"

"I got it. Thanks."

He took a step back. "Okey dokey. Will it just be you, or is Stanley coming?" A slight whine came from Sparky, who turned around and hightailed it back to the office. My dog picked up on my emotional cues. My brother did not.

"No, G, it's just me."

"Don't call me—" Seeing the look on my face, he stopped. A first for him. "So, let me know if you need anything," he finished and headed toward the office, probably to commiserate with my dog.

The store closed at five, and forty-five minutes later, the shaman arrived. He didn't look anything like I thought he would; thirties, nicely fitted jeans, a button-down jean shirt, and sneakers. Curly, shoulder-length hair framed a rugged, handsome face. Cute, but I wasn't interested. I wanted things to go back to when Stanley and I got along and had a future.

I took what my brother would call a "cleansing breath" and tried to focus. No point in upsetting myself over things I couldn't change. Plus, my brother trusted me not to let him down. I extended my hand. "Hi, I'm Ava. I'll be helping you tonight with whatever you need to facilitate the workshop."

He aimed a loose, rangy smile at me. "Hey, Ava, great place you've got here. I'm Shaman Joe."

Shaman Joe? I kept a straight face, but it required serious effort. How did my brother find these people? "How did we get so lucky to book you, Shaman Joe?"

He held on to my hand. I gave a little tug, and he put his left hand over my right. Great, now he had both my hands. I heard the door open behind me. I couldn't see who'd come in, since my hands were in a shamanic grip.

"I've known your brother awhile, and I have other friends in the area, too. There's an amazing conference going on in New Haven about ornithology right now, so I looked around to see if there were any nearby spaces for me to share my teachings. This town has a real vortex, you know?"

Hmmm. A vortex.

A voice like metal scraping against metal piped up. "I know, it really does! I'm so glad I'm not the only one who feels it!"

I stiffened. Today wasn't my day for happiness. Shaman Joe dropped my hands and waved over my shoulder. "Howdy!"

Call my brother the intuitive one, but the energy behind me was easily recognizable. "Debbee," I said through gritted teeth.

"Oh, hi," she said, blushing when I faced her. "I'm not here for you. I came for the workshop. I signed up and everything. I have my confirmation email if you need to see it."

"No need," Shaman Joe said. "Everyone is welcome here."

Shamans weren't psychic because if they were, Shaman Joe might've known I had thoughts of punching Debbee at that moment. Fortunately, I didn't act on those thoughts. The door opened and a group of people came in, happily chattering and oblivious to the rage on my face.

"We all have our journey," Shaman Joe said, looking from me to Debbee.

"Leave my dog alone," I said.

Debbee nodded. "That was wrong of me. I'll never do it again."

Shaman Joe spread his arms wide, almost knocking the display of essential oils over. "Look, healing has begun. This is going to be an amazing evening!"

"Amazing," Debbee echoed, smiling at me as if we were best friends. Could this night get any worse?

"Ava." Another voice I recognized. The answer was yes; my night could get worse. "I wasn't sure you'd be here. You didn't mention it last night, and you left kind of quick."

Great. Valdorn was here, too.

Shaman Joe smiled. "Looks like we're ready to start this party."

Chapter Thirteen

At precisely seven p.m., Shaman Joe called us back from our tea and lemonade fest. Everyone huddled in groups and talked with their friends rather than mingling. So much for the meet and greet.

One man, wearing red plaid and sporting a bushy beard, stood apart from the others. He loitered in the corner and glared at people while munching on the food I'd put out. I'd brought muffins, cookies, and cranberry nut bread to go with the tea and lemonade, and the stranger had eaten a large share of it. *Maybe he hasn't had dinner yet.* I went to welcome him, but he wasn't having it. Even Valdorn had better conversational skills. Giuseppe's workshops attracted all types of people.

"We're about to embark upon an amazing experience, not only of the spirit but of the intellect and physical body," Shaman Joe announced. I wondered at the mixture of people and whether they all expected the same experience. Somehow I didn't see grumpy plaid-shirt guy having the same experience as Debbee and Valdorn. As Shaman Joe spoke, he moved all the chairs to one side. Noticing my look—part confusion and part annoyance—he said, "It's best if we sit on the ground. This will keep us linked to Earth and facilitate our journey to the Lowerworld. Whatever we can get to help us, yes? We're doing this without the aid of traditional journey medicine, so we need to be solid in our connections."

I had no idea what he was talking about, but I smiled and nodded to let him know it was fine with me. What did I care if he wanted everyone to sit on the floor? There was carpeting, so it wasn't like they'd be sitting on a bed of rocks.

I planned to catch up with inputting new inventory into the computer system while they did whatever they were going to do. I took a few unassuming steps toward the office, smacked into something, and tripped.

I didn't entirely fall, but I did pirouette to keep my balance. Everybody gawked, though most were polite enough not to laugh out loud. *What the heck was in my way, and how did it get there?*

Sparky. He gazed at me with his beautiful, soulful eyes, trying to impart a message. *It must be dinnertime.*

"Your animal guide is urging you to stay." Shaman Joe's voice drifted through the store, harmonious and mesmerizing. Whatever.

"No," I said, adding a belated, "thank you."

"Have you ever journeyed before?" He tried to do the intense eye-contact thing with me, which was kind of cute. My brother tried that on me all the time.

"Hi, doggy." Sparky heard Debbee's voice and skedaddled. His eyes bored into me one last time before he trotted back to the office.

"You'd benefit greatly from the shamanic enlightenment happening here tonight," Shaman Joe said, still looking into my eyes. Not quite as soulful as Sparky, but adorable, in a hippie kind of way. "I sense that you can fulfill a piece of your destiny with this technique. Come, sit with us."

"I don't think—"

"Here," he said. "Across from Debbee. The contrasting energies will be good for the group. You can help lead us into the Lowerworld."

"I don't know anything about this shaman stuff," I said, desperate to get away. "Are there ghosts?"

His gentle smile encouraged me to relax. "No. No ghosts."

How bad could it be? I didn't want to be rude or make a scene. People were already gaping at me from my stunning display of grace. Might as well go and sit.

"Sometimes we do chance upon an encounter with the Masters of Outer Darkness," he went on. I almost stood back up. What the hell was a master of outer darkness? It didn't sound good, and I didn't want to see one. Nope. Not even curious. Shaman Joe sensed I was gonna bolt and came to sit next to me. He grasped my hand. "No worries, my friend. You're safe here."

Yeah, right. But it didn't matter, did it? All this Lowerworld stuff was made up and not real, so I wouldn't be in harm's way tonight. We weren't hunting a ghost, and I had a cute guy next to me. It could be fun. I looked over at the bearded grump. He scowled at me. Fun was stretching it a bit.

Shaman Joe spoke to the group. "Shamanic work in America owes a debt of gratitude to Michael Harner, the man who pioneered most of what we do today in this field." The name sounded familiar; we sold one of his books. Not that I'd read it. "The type of shamanic journey we're undertaking tonight is related to healing," he said. "Every culture has a different name for the shaman. Witch doctor, sorcerer, medicine man or woman, seer... all terms to describe the shaman. Simply put, the shaman is a guide who journeys to other places—other worlds—to help themselves or the client in some way."

A shiver ran through my body. I should've gone with the ghost-hunting gig. At least I knew what to expect with that, and I knew for a fact there was no such thing as ghosts. Probably not, at least.

"Are we using anything to aid our journey?" A tentative voice called from the back.

"Only the drum," Shaman Joe answered. "Some people use plant medicine, but we only depend on the drum."

Plant medicine? Did he mean marijuana?

Shaman Joe regarded me from extra downy eyelashes. "I don't mean marijuana. The plant medicine is usually ayahuasca."

Did he know what I was thinking? "We'll turn off the lights and leave a candle burning in the center of our circle. The candle will light our way back," he continued. *What if it blows out?* Again, as if he heard me, Shaman Joe murmured, "The candle will burn until everyone returns."

A woman in jeans and a bulky sweatshirt asked, "Where are we going? I've read that there are many worlds we can go to. Do we get to choose our destination?"

An image of a cruise ship blasted through my mind. Was Shaman Joe like a travel agent to the universe?

"It's not like we're going on a cruise," he answered, and I started. He couldn't possibly know what I was thinking.

"How many people have done this before?" he asked. Everyone except me raised their hand. "We're doing a basic journey to the Lowerworld. Do most of you have a point of entrance?" Everyone but me nodded.

He leaned toward my ear and whispered, "Imagine if you will, an entrance in nature, like a cave or a hole in a tree. Something that leads you underground. That's your point of entry."

"So imagine this," I said, gesturing around the room. Okay, I felt better. I could do this.

"Yes, picture it in your head. While I'm drumming, close your eyes and imagine the entrance. Imagine yourself jumping into the entrance and moving into the Lowerworld. You'll meet or see many strange things on your journey, but as I said, don't be afraid. You're safe here." He patted my leg.

"Like a meditation," I said, eyes growing heavy. This would be easy as long as I didn't fall asleep. Sometimes that happened when I meditated. To be honest, most times that happened.

"Think of it like that, and you'll be fine," he said. A grin flitted across his face. Wait, what was the smile for? What did he know that I didn't? He kept talking in a low, methodical rhythm, addressing the circle. "Think of the drumbeat as your canoe to carry you in and out. I start by shaking a rattle. The sound of the rattle is your cue to begin your journey. Once I've sensed all of you in the next world, I'll switch to the drum. The drumbeat sounds like this." We waited while he grabbed a small hand drum made from animal hide. He pounded a steady, rhythmic beat with his palm. "The drum carries you through your journey. When it's time to come back, you'll hear me calling you. Like this." He tripled the tempo, creating a rumble of urgency. It reminded me of summer nights when my mother hollered down the street for my brother and me to come home.

"What's our intention tonight?" Debbee asked. I tried not to look at her. I'd almost forgotten she was there. The rest of the group shouldn't have to deal with the crazy I knew lived inside her. If I didn't acknowledge her, she might stop talking and go away.

Shaman Joe beamed at her as if she were a star pupil. "Tonight we journey to claim our mission. Each of us has a purpose on this planet, and we must recognize what we're here to do. Tonight we'll begin to see a part of the path we each must walk so that we may find our way to the light."

Finally everything was ready, the lights were off, and the candle was lit. The rattling began, and I half-closed my eyes to settle in while everyone took their journey. I'd use this time to relax and decompress, take a break from the emotional mess my life had become. After five full minutes of rattling, Shaman Joe's voice broke through. "I cannot begin the next part of the journey until all of you jump into the next world."

How did he do that? Whatever. I'd have to give this a try before everyone here asked for their money back. I bit back a sigh, closed my eyes all the way, and imagined a tree with a great big hole in it. I dove into the tree and swooshed down a long, twisting slide, landing with a thud.

The rattle switched to a drumbeat.

I sat up and looked around in amazement. My imagination was working overtime on this one. The carpet of Scentsations had disappeared, and now dirt covered the ground. Trees towered over me, taller than any redwood and as big around. Bursts of color dotted the landscape, flower varieties like I'd never seen before. Each time I tried to focus on the flowers, they grew opaque, as if they didn't want to be fully seen. I raised my eyes toward the sky and found none, as the tree branches wove so tightly above me that looking up was like looking at the ground. That couldn't be right.

The drumbeat thrummed faintly, like an afterthought. I stood and brushed myself off, wondering if I could get lost in a world that I'd imagined. *She's here. She's here. She's here.* Whispers emanated from all around me. Was I hearing real whispers or a pretend someone in my pretend world?

"It's time." This voice was clear, and I peered down to see who was talking. Sparky? No, but it was a dog. Kind of like Sparky, but not Sparky. "You have to keep helping. You have to help now."

I opened my mouth to speak, and words came out even though I wasn't yet talking. It was as if my thoughts simply manifested in the air around me. "What do you mean?"

"Listen and follow. Listen and follow," the dog said. It started wandering away.

"What? Listen to what?" As I thought-said the words, the thrumming vibrated through my body. I searched for the source, walking toward where I thought I should be. The thrumming increased, becoming almost painful, and forced me forward. I ran.

I stumbled into a clearing. In the center, the earth fluttered like a heart, keeping tempo with the drumbeat. "Use your gift so that others might thrive," the dog said.

Without hesitation, I darted into the center of the clearing. *Something is here. I know it.* I clawed at the ground, frantically digging with sweat pouring down my face. I reached into the hole and pulled out a white kitten. I set the kitten aside, moving to the next area. I dug again, this time pulling a baby otter out, slick and crying. I set him aside, moving on. Each time I dug, I pulled a baby out of the earth. Kitten, otter, elephant, human. All the babies, all buried in the earth and unable to breathe. There wasn't enough time. I had to get them out…

Vaguely I grew aware of faint yet persistent drumming far away from me. The tempo was frantic, like a mother calling for her lost child. It was time to go.

"But I'm not finished," I cried.

"Go. You know what must be done now. Go," the dog said.

I looked over at not-Sparky and nodded, imagining the tree-slide I'd come down on. There it was, and there was a light at the end.

I opened my eyes. Sweat dried on my forehead and my heart raced as if I'd run a marathon. The room was dark, and the half-melted candle flickered. Shaman Joe crouched at my side. "We're glad you're back," he said. "I was starting to think you weren't coming home."

Chapter Fourteen

I felt like I had woken from a heavy sleep. What happened? Had I fallen asleep and dreamed about the buried babies? Had I drooled while I was sleeping? I put my hand on my chin, but it was dry.

"That was quite a journey," Shaman Joe said, checking in with everyone in the circle. Several people nodded, a somber air about them. "How are you?" he asked me quietly while the others started to shift and stretch.

"What was that?" I asked, reluctant to hear an answer. "I thought this was going to be like a guided meditation."

Shaman Joe remained still. I looked away. Debbee sat with her head cocked to one side, studying me as if I were a new species. She mouthed the words, "You okay?" I gave her a thumbs-up. I almost believed she cared. Her entire demeanor had changed since she'd tried to kill me. It wasn't the time to analyze Debbee's motivations. I had to clear my head.

"Let's take a short break, get some water, and then we can sit back down and review things, share some of our journeys," Shaman Joe said. Fine with me, except for sharing any of this with anyone.

"A break sounds good." The plaid-shirt guy's voice sounded ominous. He glowered in my direction. "How's business?"

I shrugged, perplexed. "Good?"

Plaid-shirt guy nodded and jutted his chin at Shaman Joe. "That's good. It's nice when your business continues… uninterrupted. When people let you get on with what you were doing."

My night was just one cryptic conversation after another.

"Are there any cookies left?" That came from Valdorn, who yawned and scratched his chest, drawing attention to his dingy Rolling Stones t-shirt.

"Whatever was left from earlier," I said, going for customer friendly. I gave it a second thought. With the plaid-shirt guy in the room, the cookies were most likely gone. Everyone meandered over to the refreshment area while I tried to wrap my head around what the shamanic journey meant and what the hell was wrong with plaid-shirt guy. Either way, my destiny included endless encounters with crazy people.

"Water will help clarify things. You should get some," Shaman Joe said. His face held nothing but kindness. We headed toward the beverages.

"I thought all this was make-believe stuff," I admitted. The part I didn't care to share, especially after what happened a couple of months ago, was my suspicions that I'd cracked. People didn't have visions. Or see an apparition of the woman who'd been murdered. But that was back in March. I hadn't seen any spirits since.

"You're not cracked," he said. He patted my shoulder and handed me a cup of lukewarm lemonade.

"There—that! How do you do that? How do you know what I'm thinking?" His constant answers to the thoughts in my head weren't helping me.

Shaman Joe laughed, a hearty laugh that struck me as down-to-earth. "I was a psych minor in college. I've learned the cues people give without intending to, and I'm clued in on body language." He leaned in conspiratorially. "I also know a little bit about you from your brother." Whatever my brother would say about me to a shaman couldn't be good. I preferred to presume it was something brotherly and annoying.

"Plus," he said when I didn't respond, "you're expressive."

Yes, that much was true. We ambled over to the lavender section, although I didn't think his chakras needed balancing. "So the place I went to wasn't my imagination? It was as if I had dropped into a real world."

"You did." Shaman Joe leaned in again, so only I'd hear. His intensity enhanced his handsome features. "The thing to remember is that the Lowerworld isn't like here. The rules are different, and the meanings of what you see are different."

"Oh, good, that clears everything up." Sarcasm, always by my side. We left the lavender oils and wandered past a few cluttered shelves of price-reduced geodes. "What do you mean by different?"

"Let's say you see a chair during your journey. The chair might be literal, or it might not. Its presence may be guiding you, encouraging you to identify what supports you in your life, as a chair supports you when you need a place to sit."

"So consider the symbolism behind what I saw." Easy enough. I tossed Shaman Joe a chunk of rose quartz.

He held it to his ear, listened intently, then put it back with the other rocks. "Yes," he said. "But it gets tricky."

Oh good. Spiritual messages cloaked in mystery. Important life lessons disguised as puzzles for me to analyze. Cool. Why couldn't we just get things handed to us on tablets with instructions? Although we'd been given instructions once, tablets with ten instructions, and that hadn't worked out well for anyone, either.

"Sometimes more information comes to us in our dreams," he continued, "and sometimes it comes in the form of a waking-dream, where information is imparted to our subconscious, and our conscious mind begins to absorb it, taking in what we need as we need it."

Everyone knew that. I nodded as if I understood what the heck he was talking about. He must've known I didn't have a clue because his following words were, "Don't worry. It will all become clear soon enough. You don't have to do anything." Big relief, there. He stopped, stretched, and said, "If you'll excuse me, I'm going outside to get some air for a moment. I need a minute to step out and decompress."

Possibly Shaman Joe was speaking code for "I'm gonna go have a cigarette." I asked him if a man at shaman-level spiritual enlightenment should be smoking.

"I'm going outside to look at the stars in the sky and offer prayers of thanks," he said. "I'll return in about five minutes."

I empathized with his need to step away from us. All of it, real or imagined, was intense.

"Ava?"

Crap-a-roni. Debbee jumped in front of me, a sheepish look in her eye.

"Yes," I said, noting the surly tone to my voice but not doing anything to change it.

"I'm sorry," Debbee said, cheeks burning. "I sort of knew something was wrong. My thoughts were odd back then. But I didn't reach out for help. And because of that, I caused harm. The doctors say that it won't happen again as long as I continue my therapy and stay on my medication. I know I have a long way to go to make it up to you, but I'm going to try."

She looked different than I remembered. Genuinely sorry, for one. Unsure of how to respond, I went with honesty. "I hear what you're saying, but it might take me a while to get over all this. You did try to kill me."

"Yeah, sorry about that. Won't happen again."

"I hope not," I said, sounding like my mother. "Let's take it one day at a time."

Debbee clasped her hands to her chest and beamed at me. "Yes, let's! So what do you think of Shaman Joe? Isn't he great? I've done this kind of thing before with him, and he's always—"

"If you'll excuse me, I told him I'd get him once his five minutes were up," I said. A small lie, but I had my fingers crossed behind my back. Although I'm not sure why that counts for anything when someone lies.

"It's okay," she said. Her shoulders slumped in disappointment. Then she brightened. "Do you need any help?"

"No, not right now. Thanks." I hurried away, grabbing Sparky so he could relieve himself outside. She was stable for now; that much was obvious. But was she trustworthy? Could I count on her not to lose it again and try to kill people, namely me? I pushed all thoughts of Debbee to the back of my mind. The answers would be more apparent later.

The back entrance was down a short hall, past the bathrooms. I pushed on the metal door and opened it slowly in case Shaman Joe stood behind it.

I stepped out into the night and a soft warmth enveloped me in the descending dusk. Spring in Connecticut is beautiful, and after a long winter—they're all long winters—everyone was ready for the new season. The air felt soft against my skin. There was no breeze, and the motion sensor light kicked on.

Not only was the air not stirring, but there were no car horns. No birds. No people talking. But most importantly, no Shaman Joe. I heard a commotion in the corner of the back parking area. *I hope those raccoons haven't gotten into the dumpster again.*

The hair on the back of my neck stood. I checked the area for any sign of our intuitive leader. He was nowhere in sight, but I knew he was back there. I could feel it, and it wasn't a good feeling. Sparky pulled on the leash, whining and then erupting into full barks.

I took a couple of careful steps into the empty lot, finding it hard to think with my dog barking like crazy. *I should go inside and get someone.* But if there was a problem, Joe needed me, and he needed me now. Everything sharpened into focus as I searched for any sign of him. *Stay aware.*

Something's wrong. "Sparky, quiet." He ignored me and kept barking.

There—the dumpster.

I suppressed a shudder and forced my legs toward the hulking pile of metal. I debated calling out his name, but my voice caught in my throat when I realized I'd also be alerting anyone else to the fact that I was out there. I needn't have worried, though, as he couldn't hear me, and no one else was out there.

Shaman Joe lay in a heap behind the dumpster, bruised and bleeding, eyes closed. Next to him, plaid-shirt guy sprawled on his side in a pool of blood, with a hole in the center of his forehead.

Chapter Fifteen

I rushed over to Shaman Joe to make sure he was alive and gasped in relief when I saw the rise and fall of his chest. "Oh God, it's okay, Joe, it's okay, you'll be okay, you're okay." I pushed down a bubble of hysteria. One minute he'd been fine; the next, he was a bloody mess. I crouched down and grasped his shoulder, hoping he'd know I was there. "I'm going to get help." Sparky whined again.

My eyes went back to the body next to Shaman Joe. I didn't need to be a detective to know that plaid-shirt guy was dead. He lay on his back, blood pooled around his head, eyes open and vacant. I knew that look, and I couldn't help him. I made the sign of the cross and turned back to Shaman Joe.

I rested my hand lightly on his chest, feeling for his heartbeat. He was breathing, so I didn't need to start CPR. Instead, I started screaming. "Help! I need some help out here!" Debbee followed me around enough to burst into Charlie's wedding planning preparations, but now she was nowhere to be found. And where the heck was Valdorn? The least he could do was drag his dirty, t-shirted self out there.

Nothing, not even birdsong. I must've frightened the local wildlife when

I screamed. Which made me wonder why we hadn't heard a gunshot. I pushed the question away. "Joe, I'll be right back. I'm going inside to get help. Stay here." Of course he'd stay there; what a stupid thing to say. I needed to hustle my heinie into the store and call the police. Why didn't I have my cell phone with me? Oh, right, we'd been sitting down. I never put it in my pocket, so it was in the office, no help to me now.

I took one last look at Shaman Joe. "Stay right there," I said again. I wanted him to hear my voice and know he wasn't alone. Except there was a dead guy next to him, but it barely counted as company.

I ran into the store. "Call the police," I gasped. "There's been an accident." I almost said *murder* but stopped myself. I didn't want to scare everybody. A lady wearing a neon-green sweatshirt whipped out her phone and started dialing. "What kind of an accident?" she asked.

"Shaman Joe and the bearded guy in the plaid shirt. They're out back. They're hurt." And one of them was dead. I hustled Sparky into the office and shut the door to keep him in there.

Everyone started talking all at once, and a few people hurried out the front door. "No, they're in the back," I said, but not too loudly. Honestly, if they didn't know front from back, they weren't of any use anyway.

Debbee approached. "What should I do?"

"I don't know," I told her. "But someone should go out back and stay with the—" I didn't want to say *dead body*. "Guys. I don't think Shaman Joe should be left alone."

She cocked her head to one side and gave me a funny look. "This wasn't an accident, was it?"

"Where are they?" questioned the lady with the phone after putting it back in her pocket.

"Did you call the police?" I asked.

She shook her head and gave a short huff. "No, I called an ambulance. You said someone was hurt."

I bit my tongue. It wasn't her fault. But we still needed the cops. I ran into the office, grabbed my phone from my purse, and sent a quick text to Oliver. He'd know what to do.

The front door bell jingled, and I hurried out, thinking that the people who had gone out were coming back in. I was wrong. It was Oliver.

"Wow, that was quick. Did you get my text?"

Oliver did a double take. "No, I was over at Big Beans. I saw some people here and thought I'd say hello. What's going on?" Big Beans was the coffee shop across the Green. It was a great place to hang out and people watch. Or wait for a catastrophe to happen so I could call and get immediate help. *Stay calm. You're in charge of this event.*

"Shaman Joe was attacked." I blurted it louder than I'd intended, and the whole room froze.

"You never said he was attacked," said one guy.

"Are you sure?" asked another.

"Where is he?" A high voice wondered.

"What kind of neighborhood is this?" interjected the lady who'd called the ambulance. Why would she ask that? Was she going to write a Yelp review?

"Did you call 911?" Oliver asked. I nodded.

Oliver assessed the room, scanning everyone. "Take me to him."

"Out back. This way." Oliver followed me through the store and past the restrooms, as did everyone else, including Debbee. We crowded at the back door. Oliver turned to address us, holding his badge in the air for everyone to see. "I need all of you to stay back, please. You can direct the emergency personnel where to go when they get here."

I spoke in a low tone so the others couldn't hear. "Oliver, it's more than the shaman. There's another man out there, and he's dead, I think. He's got a beard and a red-plaid shirt."

"Stay here. We don't know the situation yet."

"What situation? I told you."

To his credit, Oliver didn't get upset with me. "We don't know if the perpetrator is out there."

The front door jingled once more. "Police, is everyone okay?"

"Back here," Oliver called. The people dispersed, leaving room for the police officer to get through. I breathed a sigh of relief. It was Rob Genova, an old friend of mine who'd gone into law enforcement. I'd known Rob awhile, and he'd been a steady rock a couple of months ago when I needed guidance about the Ethel's murder. Rob was a strong and capable guy who exuded reliance, a quality I found comforting. Outside, sirens wailed in the distance.

"He's bleeding. We need to get to him," I said, anxious to get to Shaman Joe. I felt guilty about leaving him alone next to a dumpster. Had he lost too much blood while I went for help? His face had been a mess—had I missed a gunshot wound? Was he dying while we stood around? And what if Oliver was right and the perpetrator came back?

I shoved my way to the door. Someone grabbed hold of me and pulled me back. "This is a crime scene. Let me go first," Oliver said and pushed through to the back lot, Rob just behind him. Both their hands hovered near their weapons.

Anxious to get out there, I squeezed past the door before it shut and pointed toward the dumpster. "They're over there, on the ground," I said, voice shaking. I steeled myself for what we might find. Oliver and Rob took a few steps and stopped in front of me, not moving.

"I can't see him," I said. "Are we too late?"

"I've got eyes on the man with the beard. Where exactly was the other one?" Oliver said.

I pushed past them. "He's right here—" But he wasn't. I circled the dumpster. No Shaman Joe. "Maybe he crawled away or tried to get help." I started toward plaid-shirt guy, but Oliver held me back.

"I can't let you go any farther," he said. "We don't want you to contaminate the crime scene." He nodded to where Shaman Joe was supposed to be. Faint streaks of blood smeared the pavement, and I couldn't help but wonder if they were smeared handprints. Had the shaman tried to crawl away? Had someone dragged him away? I swallowed hard and sent out good thoughts to Joe.

"Can you find him?" I whispered. I'd only known him for a couple of hours at the most, but the guy had grown on me. He didn't deserve whatever had happened to him. And with one man already dead, Shaman Joe's chances of being found alive were slim.

A commotion near the door distracted me. "Ava!" It was Stanley and his dad, Chase.

"Ava, thank God," Stanley said.

"Ava!" My brother's wife, Janine, waved from the door, with Baby Danny tucked in her arms.

Rob ran to the door and did his best to push everyone back inside. It was no easy task.

"Ava, are you okay out there?" Debbee popped up in the doorway and flashed a tentative wave. Naturally she'd involve herself in all this.

"I need everyone to go inside," Oliver said, voice raised. "Now. We'll be inside momentarily, but if you want to help, you'll go in the store and wait." Nobody dared disobey that tone, not even Stanley.

Everyone hurried back in. I lingered behind. Shaman Joe was hurt, and he couldn't have gone far. Officers and EMTs made their way to the crime scene, and Oliver gave everyone orders. I hoped it wouldn't be long before they found Shaman Joe.

Who was plaid-shirt guy? Why had he been killed? He hadn't talked with anyone, and probably because he was too busy shoving handfuls of cranberry bread into his mouth, I hadn't heard him say his name. My brother had a registration list. We could track his name down using that.

I headed in. Stanley raced toward me, a worried look on his face. "Ava, I have to ask—"

"Hold on. I'll be right back. I'm just going to get more food." I went into the office to get more refreshments and try to get a quick peek at the computer. My brother sometimes kept registration lists on there. I found it quickly, but it was nothing more than a date and number of people. Why didn't he ask for names?

Okay, that would have to wait. For now, I had to focus on finding Shaman Joe. I grabbed more lemonade and iced tea for everyone, as well as another loaf of cranberry nut bread to slice and serve. As I was putting everything out, Stanley and Chase followed me.

"I was hoping you could—"

Janine interrupted Chase. "Ava, where's Giuseppe? What's going on here?" She stood in front of me, jiggling Baby Danny up and down. I hoped he hadn't eaten recently.

"Giuseppe is fine," I said. "He's at the ghost hunt, down in Milford. He'll be back later."

"Ava, do you know—" Stanley was interrupted again, this time by the police.

"I need everyone to take a seat and wait for us to talk to you," Rob said. "The sooner we get organized, the sooner we can get started." As Rob walked toward the front of the store, Debbee stopped him. They chatted for a moment, and Rob smiled before leading her to a corner of the room. *He's awfully friendly with someone who committed a crime not too long ago.* They talked a few moments longer, and Debbee left out the front door. Rob pulled aside a woman in pink leggings, and after a couple of minutes, she left, too.

Maybe he'd let me go next so I could start figuring this out.

"Excuse me." Chase was still trying to get my attention.

"Yes, I'm sorry. You wanted to ask me something?" I said, looking around.

Something was not quite right, but I couldn't put my finger on it. It hit me just as Chase said the very thing I'd figured out. How could I have missed this?

"We can't find Valdorn."

Chapter Sixteen

Rob asked me a couple of questions, such as where I was and what I saw, then told me I could leave. Apparently he knew where to find me. I wasn't going to go without an update, though, so I pestered him to tell me what was happening. "Where's Shaman Joe? Who is that other guy?"

"We'll get back to you as soon as we have something to tell you. In the meantime, when you see that guy… what's his name again? The one who people saw leaving earlier?"

"Valdorn."

Rob hesitated. "What kind of name is that?"

I shrugged. "He probably made it up."

"Can you spell that?" Rob asked. I spelled it out for him while he shook his head. "Yeah, when you see *Valdorn*, tell him to come on down and talk to us. We need to get everyone's timeline straight."

It was never good when law enforcement had to put together a timeline, but it was inevitable with one guy dead and another missing. "What do you think happened to Shaman Joe?" I couldn't keep the anxiety out of my voice.

"Like I told everyone, there's not much I can say right now. I'll let you know as soon as I can." He tipped his hat and left. All those words, yet Rob hadn't given me any information.

With the store finally emptied of patrons and onlookers, I had no reason to stay open. Stanley and Chase patiently waited while I locked the front door. The police locked the back door after conducting a thorough search of the store. Earlier, Janine announced that she checked her apartment above the store, and no one had crawled up to the second floor to hide in her shower stall. She offered to let Rob check for himself, but he said he had no reason to think Shaman Joe had somehow crawled up the back stairs and into her bathroom.

Still, I might check it out myself before I went home to ensure they didn't miss anything.

"Ava, I need you to go straight home." Oliver suddenly appeared at my shoulder. "Don't even think about staying here and looking for clues. I've got forensic techs who know what they're doing."

I nodded. He was right. This time I'd leave the clue finding to the professionals and find out what they knew later. "Should I give my statement?" I asked Oliver.

"We'll get it later. I know where you live." He gave me a brief smile and went to talk with the officers gathered outside.

"Can I walk you home?" Stanley asked. His boyish self-consciousness pulled at my heartstrings. Plus it was best to use the buddy system tonight. After all, a man died.

"I'm going to grab some tea," Chase called as he headed across the Green. "I'll be right back." Stanley didn't say anything but I nodded. I stood and watched him as he entered Big Beans. *I wonder if Chase likes his daughter's boyfriend.* I didn't see much to like, but it occurred to me to that I had no idea why Chase and Stanley had showed up at the store.

"Why are you here?" I asked.

Stanley pushed his glasses up his nose. "We told Valdorn we'd meet him here when your thing was done. My dad was going to bring us to get ice cream tonight."

Hmmm… so Chase must have liked Valdorn at least a little if he was willing to spring for some butter pecan. "What about your sister?"

"What about her?"

"Where is she?"

Stanley scrunched his nose. "Back home? With my mother? Why?"

Because I didn't trust her, that's why. "No reason. Just trying to sort things out in my head."

As we started down the sidewalk, Stanley said, "Do you want to come over?"

"I don't know if I should. Sparky and I might take a walk. I'm sure you and your dad—"

"We still don't know where Valdorn is, and I'd rather you had someone with you right now. It must have been an upsetting experience for you tonight."

I agreed. It'd be safer to stick with Stanley and find out more about Valdorn and where he'd disappeared to. Once inside Stanley's house, one of the night's mysteries solved itself as the missing Valdorn sat, legs splayed on the couch, eating from a tube of potato chips. Sparky huffed as if he, too, was insulted by the lump in front of us.

"Where the heck were you? We've been looking all over for you. Why did you leave?" I asked. Somebody, mainly Valdorn, was gonna give me answers tonight.

"I'm right here. Why?" His insolence stirred my anger.

The sound of the front door slamming shut echoed through the house and Chase came in. Valdorn sat up straighter on the couch. "Hey, are we getting ice cream tonight?"

"No, you're not," I snapped. "Why didn't you tell anyone you were leaving?" I thought of calling the authorities before I questioned him, but there was no turning back now. Someone had died tonight, and someone was missing, and this schmuck was shoving chips in his mouth. Not very enlightened of him.

"What are you, my mother? I was tired, so I left."

"Original," I said. "You should—"

"Ava," Chase said. "Let's not jump on Valdorn too much. He had no way of knowing what was going to happen."

I raised my hands in disgust. "How do I know what Valdorn would do? He supposedly knew you were coming to the store after the workshop, yet he left anyway."

Valdorn's eyes narrowed, his mouth twisted into a sour expression. "You're a very pushy lady."

Neither Stanley nor Chase reprimanded him. They looked in any direction but mine. I had a hunch their behavior had something to do with Victoria—sorry, *Tory*. The entire family, especially the men, seemed determined to tiptoe around her loser boyfriends so they wouldn't offend her. What did Tory's mother think of Valdorn?

I prepared to ask when Stanley took my arm. "Let's make some coffee in the kitchen."

"I'm good, I just had tea," Chase said.

I let him pull me along, and Sparky followed. Once we were in the kitchen, Stanley turned to face me and put his hands on my shoulders. "I know he's infuriating, but we're trying to keep the peace."

"I figured it had something to do with your sister."

Stanley smiled. "Yes. You've no idea how difficult she can make our lives."

My purse buzzed. I pulled my phone out and looked at it. "I have to go."

"Who is it?" Stanley asked.

"Oliver."

Chapter Seventeen

"What does he want?"

I shook my head. "Seriously? A hurt man is missing. What do you think he wants?" I didn't mention the dead guy. I sent the call to voicemail. I'd talk with Oliver later, after I got home and had time to decompress. I'd seen dead bodies before, even a murdered one, but it still left me shaken. Plaid-shirt guy was dead, and he had been lying next to Shaman Joe. None of it made sense. Who'd want to hurt a shaman? Or a bearded guy in a red plaid shirt?

Stanley paced back and forth. "I don't know, but he needs to calm down, do his job, and leave you alone."

I'd had enough. "That's priceless. You think another man should leave me alone. You should stop being clueless."

"Why are you being so…" Stanley stood in front of me, hands on hips, frowning.

"Are you really asking me that?" It had been a long night, and I wasn't sure I could handle any more of Stanley's nonchalant attitude. "Gee, Stanley, maybe you should consult Sydney about this. Maybe she'll give you some answers. In fact, maybe you could invite her to Brewster Square to stay for a while."

At that moment, Chase poked his head into the kitchen. "Do we have any more coffee, son? We might need to brew another pot if Sydney wants any."

"What?" I'd misunderstood what he'd said. Chase couldn't possibly be referring to Stanley's ex. "Do you mean Stanley's ex-girlfriend?"

Chase gave me a strange look, as if I was the one who was crazy. "Yes, you met her at the dinner."

I gaped at Chase, speechless. Stanley studied the ground. "Seriously? Is she here now?"

Chase checked his watch. "No, but she should be here within the next half hour or so. Should we put some food out or wait to see if she's had anything to eat? I think our ice cream trip is out for tonight."

A wave of emotions rushed through me. I didn't want to lose Stanley, but I didn't want to lose my dignity either. I took a deep breath and raised my chin. I pressed my hand to my thigh so my voice wouldn't waver. "I should go." I left them to their coffee-making, Sparky close by my side.

Returning home wasn't an option. I had too much energy, and besides, Sparky needed a walk. If I went home, I'd sit and stew over the events of the evening. I needed to clear my head and figure out where I was going in life and what I was doing. I started walking without purpose, uncertain and not caring about my direction, while Sparky sniffed the grass every few feet.

Slam.

Stanley's front door. The screen door always made that noise because it was old, and the hinges didn't work properly. If Stanley wanted to apologize, he'd have to do more than run after me. I turned and squinted at the house as someone power walked in the opposite direction. Not Stanley, but not Chase, either.

What the hell is he doing?

Apparently Valdorn wasn't too happy with my boyfriend—*not sure I can call him boyfriend anymore*—either. Without thinking, I pivoted and started following him.

One guy is dead, Shaman Joe is missing, and Valdorn knows something. If I follow him, I can figure out what happened to Shaman Joe. After all, the hippie weirdo disappeared right when everything happened.

I picked up my pace. This guy had something to do with it. People like Valdorn—

Tires squealed up ahead. I stepped off the sidewalk and into the shadows of a yard as a car pulled up alongside Valdorn. The passenger door swung open, and he got in without hesitation.

Questions flooded my mind, but I had no answers. I didn't know what to do. If I went back to the store, I could find something, some clue, anything that could help. *Or you'll find the people who beat on Shaman Joe, and they'll do the same thing to you that they did to plaid-shirt guy.*

My phone buzzed in my hand. Oliver again. "Hey," I said. "Valdorn got into a car with a stranger, or a stranger to me. He left Stanley's house, and this guy—"

"Ava, I need to talk to your brother."

"I know, but I think—"

"I need to talk with him now, Ava. Do you know where he is?"

His voice stopped me cold. This was serious, and Oliver wasn't messing around. "I'll call him." I pressed the End button, not caring about manners. Oliver needed to talk to G, so I'd give him a call. I dialed my brother's number and walked in the direction of his store. It was possible that with all the events of the evening he'd come back. I wasn't fooling myself, though. I wanted a chance to look at things and see if I'd missed something.

"I'm busy. Why is everyone calling me right now?" G's ragged voice registered a notch above a whisper. I rolled my eyes, glad he couldn't see me.

"I know you're busy, and I know you're ghost hunting—"

"This house is a gold mine of spirit activity," Giuseppe said. "I can't wait to listen to the tapes later. We have so much evidence here, Ava. You're not going to believe it when you hear it."

"Yeah, well, you're not going to believe this either, but I need you to come back here as soon as you can."

A dramatic exhale assailed my ear. "Seriously, can't you handle things for one night? Like I said, I'm busy. I shouldn't be on the phone right now unless it's an emergency."

Sometimes the direct approach was the only way to go with my brother. "It's an emergency. Some guy was killed behind the store. Shaman Joe was beaten, and now he's missing. The police want to talk to you."

The line crackled a moment before Giuseppe's voice exploded. "You lost Shaman Joe? How could you do that? What were you thinking?"

I winced and pulled the phone back five inches. "I didn't lose Shaman Joe. He went outside during the break, after the journey, and…" I said, trailing off. Images of his bloodied, battered body flashed through my head as I closed my eyes and tried to fight back a wave of anxiety. Everything was spiraling out of control, despite my best efforts. Tears welled in my eyes, and I hiccupped. "He… he… was bad when I found him… and then… then…"

"Okay, okay, don't worry, I'm coming. Let me get things packed up here." My brother might be all tough guy, but if I cried, he couldn't keep that act up. "Where are you?"

I sniffled before answering, wishing I had a tissue. "I'm headed to the store. Meet me there. We can go to the police station together."

"Don't—"

I pressed the End button on him. I had no interest in talking with either him or Oliver.

Sparky and I rounded the corner. Several SUVs and police cars parked haphazardly at the front of Scentsations. A crowd of bystanders milled around the area.

Debbee spotted me right away. *Why is she here?* Maybe she knew what was going on, or she had wreaked some kind of homicidal havoc again. I gave her a short wave and asked, "Did someone forget to invite me to the party?"

"I'm here to see if they found anything." Debbee's excitement made me instantly wary. If Debbee was excited, it couldn't mean anything good.

"If who found anything? Is this about what happened tonight?"

Debbee nodded and gestured to the parked SUVs. "It's the local SAR group."

I had no idea what she was talking about, so I ignored her. Rob stepped out of a police car and jogged our way. "Ava, do you know where your brother is? Oliver's looking for him."

"He's on his way back from a ghost hunt," I said. "I called to let him know we needed him here. What's all this?"

Rob, Debbee, and I assessed the busy scene. I heard barking. "It's the canine SAR folks," Rob said. Debbie clapped her hands.

Rob and Debbee were in the know, and I wasn't. "Who?"

"SAR: search and rescue," Rob said. "We brought the dogs in."

Chapter Eighteen

Sparky perked up at the promise of some new canine companions, but many handlers were putting the dogs back in their vehicles. Apparently in urban settings there can sometimes be too many scents and the dogs couldn't get a real sense of which way someone went. I wanted to argue that we were more suburban than urban, but I snapped my mouth shut in the face of all those official-looking people. Everyone wore a uniform of some type or other, and they all appeared very efficient.

"So now what?" I asked Rob. "If the dogs go home, is that it?"

"Oh, no, not at all," Debbee answered breathlessly. I held back a sigh. What did she know about tracking scent? "I trained with SAR before, well, you know."

"Before you tried to kill me?" The words flew out of my mouth. At least she looked repentant. "Why are they here now? Why weren't they here when the police first got here?"

"Because they're volunteers," Rob said. I looked at the group again, more confused than ever.

"Volunteers? In uniform? With dogs? How does this work?"

"It's wonderful," Debbee said. "These folks work as a team with their dog, training together every week. When they get called out, they all go—well, whoever is available goes—and participate in the search. Some SAR teams don't use dogs, but they all have one thing in common. They save lives. The work is quite extensive." Debbee waved her arm around her as she spoke. I stepped out of the way of all the enthusiasm.

As annoying as her eagerness was, she seemed to know a lot about search and rescue. "None of them are with the police department?"

"No, we call on them when the state police can't respond, or when we need more searchers," Rob answered. "Oliver's here. You should talk to him."

Oliver walked toward us with long, competent strides. His face masked his thoughts. I hadn't seen this look on him since—

Since Ethel died.

A shiver ran up my spine. Oliver and I may have started out rocky, but that was because he'd acted like a horse's ass. He'd been doing his job, but he didn't have to be so rigid and formal and generally difficult. I'd only been trying to help.

"Ava, is your brother here yet?"

"Hello Oliver, I'm fine, despite finding a dead guy tonight, thanks for asking." Oliver didn't respond. I sighed and continued. "He's on his way. He should be here in about twenty or thirty minutes, coming from Milford."

"And you're sure he's coming?"

"As sure as I can be about anything related to my brother. Why do you want to talk to him? Do you think he knows anything about Shaman Joe? Did you find him? Are you still looking? Because frankly, it looks to me like you've got a whole bunch of people standing around here. What about the murdered guy?" The more I spoke, the angrier I became. I wasn't getting a real sense of urgency from anyone.

"We're actively investigating his disappearance, as well as the incident tonight," Oliver said. "Do you know of any family Joe might have in the area?"

I had no idea. I looked at Debbee, whose eyes had gone wide. She gave a slight shrug. "It was a shamanic workshop, not a genealogy class," I said. Oliver glared at me like I should know the guy's cousins and aunts. "As I told you earlier, I met the guy tonight. What's up with these dog folks? Do you need something that belonged to Shaman Joe so they can find him?"

Oliver gave me a small smile, which brought an inexplicable sense of relief. I didn't like it when he went into cop-mode with me. "They aren't that kind of dog. They follow the scent trail of whoever was here last. They can pick up human scent anywhere in the vicinity."

Sparky barked and play-bowed at a German shepherd who walked in front of us with its owner. "Sparky, I don't think he wants to play with you. He has a job to do," I said as my dog wiggled his butt. I swear the shepherd gave my dog a nod when he walked by. It had been a long night; maybe I was hallucinating.

"See, his handler took the vest off, so the dog knows he's not working," Debbee said.

"You speak, and yet I have no idea what your words mean." It was snarky, and I regretted it. It wasn't right to take it out on her. Even if she was a lunatic. "I'm sorry," I said. "It's been a long day."

"I understand about having bad days," Debbee said. "It happens to me, too, if I forget to take my meds."

"So you're going to walk out on my brother?" An angry voice cut through the air, and I cringed.

"Tory. How are you?" I turned in her direction. I didn't know she would be coming to Brewster Square, too. Maybe she rode with Sydney. "When did you get here?"

"Not that it's any of your business, but I've been here since late this afternoon and did some shopping… you know what, not your business. Besides, what the hell? When I got to his house, my brother said you left in a huff and weren't coming back. That's not cool, you know. You can't treat him like that."

Time to set the record straight. "I left because I didn't feel like being jerked around anymore."

Right on cue, a sneer crossed her face. "My brother doesn't jerk people around. He's the one who ends up getting hurt every time."

"Don't worry; he's found a way to heal those hurts. Why don't you hurry back to his place? You'll have time to sit and visit with Sydney." Her face whitened, and I knew she had no idea. "Oh, didn't you know? Ever since their little reunion at the dinner, Stanley and Sydney have been closer than ever." This time I didn't regret my snark. It was hard-earned.

"Seriously? After what she did to him?" Tory returned to her usual look: disgusted at the world. "I'm looking for Valdorn. Where is he?" So I wasn't going to get much from her in the way of sisterly camaraderie.

"He jumped in someone's car and left," I said and pointed at Oliver. "They were looking for him earlier. I told the police, but nobody seemed to care that some vehicle sped up next to him, opened the back door, and he got in. I told them it looked weird—"

"No, it's fine." Tory backed away from us. "I'll… I'll catch up with him later. I know those guys. They're friends. Just friends. Bye." She spun around and hurried off.

"Who are these friends?" I called.

"Nobody." She waved her arm in the air, not even bothering to turn around. "See you later."

I knew it. Something weird was going on with that freak boyfriend of hers. And why had she shown up unannounced? Oliver's voice cut through my thoughts. "Ava, you need to come to the station with me."

"Now?" I asked. Even Debbee's eyebrows raised. "Sparky's with me. I didn't think he was allowed in there. You said we could talk later."

"Yes, now. And call your brother again and tell him he needs to hustle down here. I need to see him at the station immediately. If he can't—or won't—be there, I'll issue a warrant for his arrest."

"Do you want me to come with you?" Debbee asked.

I shook my head. I didn't want to bother my mother, but I had to call her. And Charlie. I needed reinforcements.

CHAPTER NINETEEN

I brought Sparky home and got him into his crate without much fuss. He liked being in the crate when his favorite toys were in there. That dog played more than any dog I'd ever known, which I supposed was a good thing. He tossed his plastic bone in the air and caught it as I secured the crate door, giving me a look that said, "See, I can amuse myself." Or it was, "Don't be too long, or I'll destroy this toy." Hard to know.

My mother said she'd meet me at the police station as soon as possible and not to worry; she'd pick up Charlie on the way. I knew I could always count on those two women to be there when I needed it, like my aunts. I didn't want to bother them at this time of night, though, so I hadn't called the aunts.

Some habits are harder to break than others, I thought as I listened to the phone ring. Without thinking, I'd dialed Stanley's number. What I thought I'd accomplish was a mystery even to me.

"Hello?" It wasn't Stanley's voice.

"I apologize. I think I called the wrong number."

"Are you looking for Stanley?"

My heart sank. I didn't even need to ask. "Sydney?"

"Yes, dear?"

She knew it was me. I hated that kind of thing. Plus, I wasn't any good at it. Then the anger came. "I'm not sure what it is you think you're doing, but have fun. I hope you're happy in your world of lies. I'm sure Stanley will wake up one day and regret this, but it's his choice, not mine." I hung up. Whatever they were doing, or thinking about doing, was their business. I was officially done with Stanley.

My phone rang in my hand, causing me to jump a little. I took ten steps, hoping that by moving, I could delay the inevitable. I pushed the Answer button but didn't speak. I had nothing to say.

"Ava? Ava, I know you're there."

I walked in a large circle around my living room, taking twenty-five steps and still not talking.

"Ava, I can explain. She's only here—"

"Please don't call me again. I think we're finished. I don't want to see you anymore. Good luck with whatever you do." I ended the call and immediately felt lighter. Time to move on. I went downstairs and out the front door, counting my steps as I went. I took a deep breath and threw my shoulders back. A mixture of anger and sadness swirled through me, but I pushed it all away. It was time to see Oliver at the police station.

"Why are you sticking your chest out?" Debbee asked, coming from out of nowhere and startling me.

"I'm not. I'm correcting my posture. And standing up for myself."

"But you're already standing. Walking, actually."

I rolled my eyes. "Why are you following me?" Oddly, I didn't feel threatened or annoyed, which I'd have to consider later. A medicated Debbee seemed like a regular, nonthreatening woman. What if she forgot to take her meds one day, though?

"I have to go to the police station, and you're going in the same direction. I thought we could walk together."

I shrugged, noncommittal. If she didn't do anything weird, I'd walk with her. I didn't have the energy to argue.

My brother would be at the police station by now. I'd ask him about plaid-shirt guy. I was tired of thinking of him as "plaid-shirt guy." He deserved better than that. Did he have family waiting for him to come home? Did he have a wife and kids somewhere who'd be devastated to learn he'd died?

It didn't take long to walk to the police station from my house. We crossed the town green, fashioned in a typical New England style. The large square of grass, which was common to most small New England towns, had a gazebo smack in the middle of the Green. Each corner of the square boasted a giant bronze horse and rider statue. They were supposed to be soldiers, but to me, they looked like the four horsemen of the apocalypse. Buildings and businesses sat side by side around the Green, including old houses with tons of character and charm. We walked down Church Street, turned the corner of the Green onto Academy, then took a right onto Pine Road, mainly in silence.

What the heck was I doing? I was worried sick about a man I'd just met, not too worried about a hippie who may have been kidnapped, and steaming mad at a man I'd just dumped. Plus, I was heartsick at another death. All in under twenty-four hours. A new record for me.

Somebody touched my arm. "We're here," Debbee said. I glared at her, causing her to take a step back. Boy, I was in a mood.

We went into the police station and approached the window. Every time I had been in there, I wanted to talk loudly so the person on the other side could hear me. "We're here to see Oliver," I announced.

The man behind the window ignored me and stared at his computer. He was a large man with thinning dark hair and a mustache. I couldn't see his name tag, and I didn't recognize him. I huffed. He was probably checking his Facebook status. Finally, he glanced up at my frowning face.

"You're here for what?" he intoned.

"To see Oliver," I said, enunciating each word and speaking louder. I still wasn't convinced he could hear me.

"I can hear you fine. Do you mean Detective Rialto?"

Before I could answer with any snark, Debbee stepped closer and said, "Yes, he requested that we come down to answer a few questions."

The officer picked up a phone and spoke into it, but I couldn't hear what he said, proving my point that the clear plastic divider between us muffled sound. "He'll be right out. Why don't you have a seat over there?" He pointed at some boxy wooden chairs with ratty gray upholstery.

We walked over, but neither of us sat. Debbee shrugged and plunked herself into the nearest chair. I preferred to stand, and not just because of the dubious stains. Weird energy thrummed through me. I'd been awake for too long, and I suspected my emotions were in overdrive. I couldn't sit still, so I paced a little, counting steps as I walked.

A few minutes later, as I tired of counting the same twelve steps, Oliver came through the door that led to the inner offices. He nodded once and said to Debbee, "Let's get you back there first." To me, he added, "This won't take long. I'll be right out." The door swung shut before I could formulate a thought. *He must be in a hurry to move this case forward.*

I wandered around the waiting area, picking up various brochures and reading them. *Is That House a Drug House* and *Is The House Next Door Used for Trafficking* were my two favorites, even if they mostly had the same information. I'd thought that having a drug house in the neighborhood was more a matter of bad luck than strategy, but it turns out, no, drug houses worked like any other business. Drug and trafficking houses might have barred or opaque windows and people acting suspiciously at all hours of the day. *They need a new copywriter.* Even in my limited experience, I knew there was more to the trafficking issue than barred windows.

I'd reached for the brochure titled, *Trafficking: It's Not Just People*, which was sure to be a thriller, when my mother and Charlie burst through the door, speaking at the same time. "What happened? Did you get hurt?"

I hugged them both before I answered. "I'm fine. It's been a long day. Night. Whatever. I found a body in the back parking lot. I have no idea who he is. Big guy, beard, plaid shirt. And the shaman guy is missing, too. I'm worried something horrible happened to him. Oliver seems to be anxious to find him, which is why I think he asked me to come here. And I broke up with Stanley." I tried to add that last bit in casually, but they gasped in unison, their mouths tiny matching O's.

Charlie spoke first. "What happened?" I loved that she skipped the entire dead person/missing person issue and went straight to the boyfriend drama. Ex-boyfriend, now.

Sooner or later I'd have to explain it in its entirety, but for now, broad strokes. "His girlfriend. I'll explain it later. I need to finish here, go home, get some sleep, and help find Shaman Joe tomorrow. And figure out who that person was who died tonight." *Don't cry, don't cry, don't cry.* "I hope he didn't have kids who are waiting at home for him."

My mother reached into her purse and handed me a tissue. "That sounds like a good plan. Giuseppe probably knows who this man was. What have they done so far to find the shaman?"

"They had dogs at the store, but they said they couldn't use them because," I scrunched up my face, trying to remember the reason, "it was too scented?" I still didn't know why they couldn't set the dogs loose. The clock was ticking, and we didn't have time to be picky. I didn't get into it further because the door opened, and Oliver and Debbee walked out.

"Let me know if anything changes," he said to her before turning to me. "Come on back, Ava, let's get you started." He held the door open and waited while I hugged my mother and Charlie again.

"G is on his way here," I told my mom. "Can you wait for him?"

"Of course. You're my children." She glared at Oliver as if realizing for the first time that he might pose some sort of threat to her babies. In return, his weak smile told me he understood her mama bear look and was anxious to get out of the way. Nobody wanted to get between my mom and her children when she got all defensive. We were lucky—she protected us with scary ferocity. For good measure, she threw one of those looks at Debbee, who scuttled out the door quickly with a short wave.

I followed Oliver back to his office and tried to clear my thoughts of Stanley. He didn't deserve to take up any space in my head. At the doorway, Oliver stepped aside and ushered me in ahead of him. I took a seat at the chair in front of his desk and checked out the decor with interest. Everything was neat and in order, with no papers scattered around. A cactus sat on the edge of the desk, complete with a bright pink flower. His file cabinets had a variety of other cacti, many of them blooming and all gorgeous. He had no personal pictures that I could see, and a whiteboard hung on the wall with a list of open cases and names. I tried to decipher what the letters and numbers meant on the board.

"Don't try to figure it out," he said.

I sat back. "What do you need to know? I'm not sure of exact times—"

"Hold on a moment." Oliver sat carefully in his chair, opened a desk drawer, and pulled out a recording device. "Do you mind if I tape this interview?"

I froze. Taping an interview meant he thought I knew more than I did, but I wasn't sure what. "I don't think I have a choice, do I?"

Oliver didn't answer my question. He turned the device on and spoke the date and our names before starting. "I want you to tell me in your own words everything you know about the deceased man you found, and then I want you to tell me about your brother's store and how this shaman person came to be teaching a class there."

I relaxed a bit. This would help. I detailed the evening to Oliver and ended with, "I don't know where G finds these people. I guess they must network with each other somehow."

Oliver shook his head. "You shouldn't call him G. Let's back up for a minute. I need to ask you details about your brother's store. Tell me about his ordering system. Where does he get his merchandise?"

I leaned back in my chair and narrowed my eyes. What did this have to do with a murdered man? Any little clue could break a case wide open, but his questions seemed to have taken an abrupt turn. "You need to tell me why you threatened to arrest my brother."

Oliver ran a hand through his hair. "I don't need to tell you anything. But I will tell you, unofficially, that we believe we know the identity of the man who was shot. An officer recognized him but until I confirm it with your brother, I cannot say his name."

"Is that why you want to talk to my brother?" I waited. Oliver had questions, but I wasn't answering any of them until I knew if my brother was in trouble.

"While I'm convinced your brother isn't involved in what we're investigating, I need to know details about his store. The crimes tonight might be tied to something bigger."

Oliver always told the truth. I had no doubts about him, so I relayed everything I knew about my brother's system and answered questions about his online ordering. But one thing bothered me. "How come I didn't know someone had been shot?"

Oliver looked at me sharply. "What do you mean?"

"Shouldn't I have heard something? A gunshot or a struggle or something?"

His shoulders dropped. "Not necessarily. People tend to get quiet when a gun is pointed at them. And if the perp used a silencer, you wouldn't hear anything." He hesitated for a moment. "Ava, none of what happened tonight is your fault."

I shrugged. "I should've known someone was being killed back there."

It was late, I was tired, and I wanted to go home to my dog. Finally, he turned the recorder off. "It's late. Go home. We'll talk later."

I didn't need to be told twice.

Chapter Twenty

A bright light surrounded the tall man, making it hard for me to see him clearly. He could've been any age. His long hair was tied back in a ponytail, and he offered me a kindly, wistful smile. "You must seek our shaman," he said.

Everything was different here, and I couldn't figure out where I was. "Who are you?"

"I am of the place you visited. We are meeting here, in the in-between, the dreamplace."

I remembered Shaman Joe's words: *sometimes information comes to us in our dreams*. "Is this about Shaman Joe's disappearance?"

The man nodded. "He can help you, and you can help us."

"Someone else was there tonight, someone who died. Do you know that man?"

Everything blurred, and the man in front of me broke apart like static. "He's not... us... cannot..." His voice faded, and the light flared once briefly before extinguishing.

Slam. Crash.
Thump thump thump thump.
Slam. Crash.
Thump thump thump thump.

I opened my eyes to weak sunlight filtering into the bedroom and a wet nose with a rubber ball. Sparky grabbed the ball, ran out of the room, smashed into something, and ran back in with the ball, proudly dumping it next to me on the bed. I loved my dog, but all he wanted to do was play. All. The. Time.

Sunday mornings should be quiet, relaxed affairs. Instead, I awoke with a sense of dread and the feeling that time was ticking. I squinted at the clock next to the bed. Six o'clock in the morning. I lay still for a moment, contemplating my dream. Was someone trying to reach me and give me a message about Joe? I sighed. That sounded kind of silly.

Coffee was most definitely in order. After two cups and a long walk around the Green, Sparky and I returned home to start our day. Oliver knew more than he was telling me, but maybe there was some way I could learn what he knew. Or what he was trying to find. Or who he might still care about. *It doesn't matter. We're not involved in that way.*

That kind of thinking was futile. I wouldn't get answers until Oliver wanted me to have them. He'd been an undercover agent, for crying out loud. What made me think he'd tell me anything at all?

I took a quick shower and tried to formulate a plan for the day. I needed to check in with my brother and find out what had happened with him last night. If I stopped by his house to see him, I had to make sure it didn't coincide with mealtime.

Sparky selected another toy and ran with it from one room to the next. My cell phone rang, and the readout on the screen said it was Aunt Maria. "Incoming," she said when I answered. My heart sank. This early? It was only eight in the morning.

"Do you know who it is?"

"Older guy, gray hair, well-dressed. Looks like a grown-up version of Stanley."

Crapcrapcrapcrap. "Okay, thanks."

"You need me up there?"

I smiled. I could always count on my aunts in any situation, no matter what. "No, I'm good. Thanks."

"Before you go, I need to talk to you about your dog," she said.

"Did he eat something of yours?" Perhaps he'd snuck down and chewed on a shoe or purse or couch or something.

"No, but I hear him playing every day."

"I'm sorry, I'll try to keep him quiet. I didn't mean to bother you."

"He's not a bother at all, but you should consider—" I missed the end of her sentence over the sharp rapping on my door.

"Aunt Maria, he's here. Can we talk later?"

"Yes, dear. See me when you have time."

I opened the door to a disheveled Chase. He looked tired and worn out and probably hadn't taken the time to identify a single bird on the way over. I steeled myself against a sudden sadness. We were tied only by my tenuous connection to his son.

Chase tucked in his shirt and tried to put himself together. "I need your help."

I nodded. Chase needed me to help him. Sure. "Come in." Win's words ran through my mind. I had to be cautious. Stanley had shown himself to be less than trustworthy, so it was likely his father was the same. *That's not fair. Give him a chance to talk before you judge him.* Great. My inner critic, siding with my ex's father.

Chase strode straight to the windows overlooking the town green. I let him gather his thoughts. Finally, he turned to me. "My wife and I are fully aware that our daughter is a screwup.”

His words hung in the air. I was stunned. What kind of father said something like that to someone he barely knew?

He sighed. “Here's the thing. I love Victoria, but she makes some questionable life choices. Still, I don't want to see her hurt. And this entire situation here has me concerned. I don't care if I never see that weirdo hippie boyfriend of hers again, but he's gone missing, and so has that other person, and someone else is dead. I need Valdorn found so he and my daughter can leave town and go somewhere safe.”

I agreed with him on all points. When I nodded, he continued. “From what I can see, you're a smart woman. Stanley told us a little about what happened recently with that woman who died.”

“Us?” I interrupted. I could only imagine who he meant with that all-inclusive pronoun.

“Yes, Birdie and I.” A momentary look of confusion crossed his face, quickly replaced by the original fatigued look. “Like I said, I need your help. We need your help.”

Oh boy. “We?”

The confused look returned. “Birdie and I.”

“I'm not sure what I can do to help you.”

Chase took a deep breath. He walked away from the window toward the sofa and turned to me, running a hand through his hair. “Talk to the police. See if they have any leads. You know this town—where would Valdorn disappear to? Who would he run off with? If he did run off.”

I shook my head. “Nope. No can do. Not me. I'm sorry. Have a nice day.” No way would I get involved in Stanley's family affairs. “Talk to Stanley. I can't help you. Someone died last night. What you're asking me to do could be dangerous.” There. That last sentence should shut him down.

Chase stood as still as he had when he watched birds. “Does this hesitation of your have anything to do with Sydney?”

My stomach dropped. It was about Sydney. "No. I don't think I need to be involved in a police matter." *Besides*, I added silently, *don't you care about my safety?* It didn't matter that I had plans of my own, plans that involved helping not only Shaman Joe but also my brother, who for whatever reason had gotten dragged into this. My brother was family; Chase was not.

"I understand you feel threatened by Sydney, but they never stay together, even if Birdie might expect them to marry someday."

"That's news to me," I said, throwing him a look that told him what I thought of that idea. "And I don't care. Stanley and I are no longer a couple." My true feelings were none of his business.

Chase stared at me for a moment. "You broke up with him? Why did you do that?"

Seriously? He had to ask? "Because Stanley hasn't been honest with me. We had an agreement always to tell each other the truth. He has unresolved issues with Sydney that he needs to clear up."

He waved his hand in the air as if it didn't matter. "They do this all the time. You've got to ignore them."

Tired of debating my relationship status, I changed the subject. "Why do you think I should be the one to look into this instead of your son?"

Chase paced to the window again and kept his back to me. "I don't think Stanley can handle this kind of thing. He doesn't have the right approach. If you keep your head down, you'll be perfectly safe."

You can't even look at me right now while asking me for this big favor. "You underestimate your son," I said. "He's the mayor. He has his finger on the pulse of everything that happens here. Everyone knows him."

"Exactly," Chase interrupted, finally turning to face me. "Everyone knows him, so he needs to stay out of it. To protect his political interests."

He strode toward my kitchen, reached into his jacket pocket, and pulled out a business card. After placing it on my table, he turned to me. "Think about it and call me. I only need you to find Valdorn. That's it. I can pay you. Five hundred dollars." With that, he walked out the door.

Five hundred dollars? Was he serious? I stared at the card for a moment, Win Thurgood's words ringing in my head. *That man is not to be trusted.*

Chapter Twenty-One

Chase was right. In fact, with Oliver harassing my brother and Shaman Joe still missing, I'd take some sort of action anyway. I paced from one end of my apartment to the other, counting steps and thinking about what to do first. *One, two, three, four…* Who were Shaman Joe's friends? How did Giuseppe know him? *Seventeen, eighteen, nineteen…* What was the dead man's identity, and why was he killed? Did Valdorn know him? Once I reached twenty-five, which was the end, I turned to go the other way and began again. *One, two…* Why did Oliver insist on dragging my brother to the station to discuss his retail business? What did Scentsations have to do with anything? My brother couldn't have been linked to the disappearance because he'd been in Milford. And his store sold harmless things, oils and geodes and books. Who'd want to hurt a shaman? *Nine, ten, eleven…*

I stopped short. Shaman Joe was sweet and kind, but Valdorn wasn't. I could easily see plenty of folks not liking him. Were the disappearances connected?

So much had happened in such a short amount of time, and I had to take action. I could use the excuse that I'd never had a chance to meet with Oliver for dinner once I returned from Stonington. *No time like the present.*

I picked up my phone to send him a text.

Hello!

I waited for an answer but got nothing. How much time was acceptable before I sent another text? After five minutes, I sent another. I'd be reasonable. I wouldn't bug him.

Call when you get a chance. Bye!

If he didn't answer my text, I'd have to be proactive and visit him at work. But I'd give him some time to respond. My first stop would be to see Giuseppe at work.

A few customers were in Scentsations when I arrived, but I could tell they were browsing and wouldn't make any purchases. Giuseppe sat on a stool behind the counter with one hand on the cash register and one on his knee. Both palms were up, and his eyes were closed. He was either meditating or sleeping.

"Hey, G, I need to talk to you," I said in a hushed tone. Despite using my inside voice, he jumped as if I'd poked him.

"Don't call me that." He arched his back to stretch and ran his hand through his hair. "What's up? You're not on the schedule for today."

I looked a little more closely at him. He hadn't shaved, and there were circles under his eyes. "That was a late night. How long did Oliver keep you there?"

He nodded and reached for his Hydro Flask. "I don't know. I got home around three or four. He had a ton of questions."

My first thought was *what the hell, Oliver*, but quickly changed to a more subdued version. *I hope it helped.* "Were you able to tell him anything useful? Do they have any leads on Shaman Joe? Do you know who that man was who died?"

Giuseppe shook his head. "No. I answered all his questions, even the stupid ones, but I don't think I was any help."

"Stupid questions? What do you mean? What did he ask you?"

"He asked a lot of things I expected, like how did I know Joe and how did I meet him, and did I know any of his friends. Then he started asking me about the places Joe traveled to and the types of things he did when he traveled. How am I supposed to know that stuff? And he asked how many languages I spoke."

Giuseppe stopped, and we looked at each other. Both of us knew it wasn't a good sign. "What now?" I asked.

He looked at the floor. I knew what that meant. It meant my big brother thought he needed to protect me, so he wasn't going to ask for my help. "Too bad," I said.

"Too bad what?"

"Too bad you think you're protecting me by not asking for my help because I'm going to help anyway."

"You should stay out of this one, Sis." Giuseppe stood and straightened some items on the counter. "No offense, but there's not much you can do." He ran his hand through his hair again. "Let the police handle it."

I studied him. "What aren't you telling me? Why are you so mopey?"

"I'm not mopey. But I'll answer one of your questions. The man who died was named Quinn. I checked the registration list, and he's the only person not accounted for. Oliver and I went through the list together last night." At that point he yawned, and not the delicate kind.

"You look exhausted." What were sisters for if they couldn't be complimentary, right?

"I am exhausted. It's not only Quinn's murder or the disappearance of Shaman Joe. It's the house preparations."

That didn't make much sense to me, but this was my brother, after all. "You mean packing? I'm going to start saving all the boxes."

"Not that, but I guess we're going to have to pack, too," he said. "I'm putting together herb bundles so we can begin the purification process for the new house. I know we're going to need powerful rituals to cleanse the structure, so I'm beginning the preparations."

It was difficult to know what my brother was talking about on a good day. Today, I didn't want to know. "Anyway, have you heard anything about Shaman Joe or where he went? He seemed like a nice guy." If he hadn't forced me to participate in his class, I'd like him even more. At any rate, he was kind, which meant a lot to me. "And thanks for telling me about Quinn." *Now I don't have to think of him as plaid-shirt guy.* "Do you know anything about him?"

Giuseppe shook his head. "Not really. I've seen him around, but he was always alone, and he, well, I don't mean to sound judgmental."

Every time someone says they don't mean to sound judgmental, it means they're about to serve up a heaping pile of judgment. I mitigated his guilt. "At this point, you're just sharing information."

"Yeah, well, he never seemed like a nice guy. I know that sounds harsh, but he was always a bit abrupt. Sort of rude."

I nodded. "I saw that, too."

"I don't know what happened to the shaman, but I hope they figure it out soon," Giuseppe said. "I met him years ago, back when he went by 'Joe' and before he started hanging out in South America."

"Wait, what? South America?" No wonder Oliver was curious about all that. Now I was, too. "Why did he hang out in South America?"

Giuseppe squinted at me. "He's a shaman; why wouldn't he?"

Like that made any sense. I needed to ask different questions. "How did he get to be a shaman? Did he take a class or read about it or... how does someone get to be a shaman?" This wasn't an idle question—I was genuinely curious. How on earth does one choose that career path?

"Do you remember my friend Jacob?"

I had a vague recollection. "Didn't he marry that woman, the short one with the dark hair?"

My brother nodded. "Not the best description, but yes. Her name is Maya. They got Joe involved in shamanism. They've spent years studying with some of the most amazing elders."

"How did Shaman Joe know Jacob and Maya?"

Giuseppe sighed. "I'm trying to tell you that. Joe lived in New Haven for a little while. He met Jacob and Maya through an artist's co-op, and they started working together."

"Shaman Joe's an artist?"

"Will you stop interrupting me!"

"I'm trying to get the story straight. How does Quinn fit into all this? Was he a friend, too?"

"Yes, but not directly. Although Quinn knew most of the elders, too, because I remember him being at this one event at Jacob's house. But he wasn't—"

"How can you not be a direct friend? Either you're a friend or you're not."

"If you'd let me tell you, then you'd get it straight."

The bell on the entrance door jingled as someone either came or left. "I am letting you tell it, but you get all involved in these side stories about elders and—"

"That's part of the story!"

"I doubt it. Every time you tell—"

"Children!" Our mother's voice still had the power to make us stand straight and stop talking. "What are you arguing about?"

"Nothing," we echoed.

"Nothing?" she asked, waving her hands around. My mother always talked with her hands. "I come in here, and my two children are sniping at each other. Remember, you're lucky to have each other because—"

"Family is everything," Giuseppe and I said in unison, smiling.

"You're right, Mom," I said. "We both had a long night, but that's no excuse."

"I'm exhausted," Giuseppe said. "And you're right, Ava, I got sidetracked."

"Sidetracked about what?" My mother maneuvered around me and plunked her purse behind the counter.

"What are you doing?" I asked.

"I'm here to work. Giuseppe has too much going on right now to be here, so I thought I'd step in and help."

We thought about this. "You think I can't do the job?" my mother asked.

"You can do the job!" Giuseppe said a little too heartily. "You can do a great job. I'm not sure why you're here."

"Janine called." My mother rummaged through the items under the cash register, bending down to look for God knew what. "She's a mess right now, trying to get ready for the move and have all the papers in order for the mortgage company and what with little Danny choking on a hot dog."

"What the hell!" I yelped. A hot dog?

Giuseppe shot me a look. "Calm down. We only give him tofu dogs." My brother yawned again. "Yeah, that happened two days ago. I don't know why she's worried about it now."

"Because she's a mom," I said. Janine was an amazing mother and person. I hoped my brother knew how lucky he was. "Anyway, I'll let you get to it. I'm sure you have lots going on with the move and all. Let me know what I can do to help and when moving day is." I stepped behind the counter and kissed my mother on the cheek. "I'll talk to you both later."

"Where do you think you're going?" my mother asked.

Crap. I wasn't going to tell her what I was up to since she'd have a fit. "Errands." Technically it was true, but not the kind of errands that involved picking up milk.

"It's such a nice day out. I thought you could come out for a visit and dinner later. We can eat outside," my mother said. "Maybe around six?

Your father would love to see you. We worry, you know."

Naturally they worried. Every parent worried, but I had the added benefit of a mother who provided food each time she worried. Good food. "I'd love to. What's for dinner? Should I bring something?"

"No, just show up. Your father is working on his tractor today, so he'll be home all day. We're having stuffed manicotti, salad, and garlic bread. Oh, and antipasto. Giuseppe, you should come too. Janine doesn't have to cook tonight."

"Okay, Ma." My mother's cooking was the one exception Giuseppe made to the food he gave his kid. Her mom-magic made up for any chemicals that might dare sneak into the pasta.

As I headed for the door, my mother called out, "Ava, be careful. Don't get involved in what's going on."

No answer was better than a promise I couldn't keep.

Chapter Twenty-Two

The bright sunshine was nice, but it didn't match my mood. The world had gone off-kilter and a cloudy day would have been a better reflection of this. How could it be a pleasant spring day when people were dead and missing? At the police station, a different person sat behind the plexiglass. This time he buzzed me right through. I heard the clicking of someone typing on a keyboard, but other than that, the back offices seemed deserted. I found my way to Oliver's office and peeked in. He had the same exhausted, harried look as my brother. "How's it going?" I asked.

He looked up and stood from behind his desk. "Fine. What brings you here this morning?"

I took the lone seat across from him. "You never answered my text. I thought I'd stop by and see if you wanted to have lunch."

Oliver sat again and studied me for a beat, making my heart race. Why was he looking at me like that? He hadn't given me that look since back when I'd been trying to figure out who killed Ethel. "Why are you here? Stanley couldn't tell you anything?"

"I don't know what Stanley can or cannot tell me." I fought to maintain my composure. "Stanley and I aren't exactly speaking."

"Why was his father visiting you this morning?"

It didn't surprise me that he knew about that. He'd seen Chase outside my building this morning. Lots of people probably saw him this morning and wondered. Brewster Square was a small town; Oliver wouldn't be the only person to ask me about my visitor. "He wanted to talk to me about Stanley and Tory. And Sydney."

He rubbed his chin. "Who's Sydney?"

"Stanley's girlfriend."

His eyes widened. I'd shocked him. He leaned back in his chair. "I'm sorry. When did that happen?"

"I had the pleasure of meeting her in Stonington at his parents' anniversary dinner." I related the minimum amount of information to avoid any emotional meltdown. "They've been a thing all along. Longer. Maybe forever. I don't know."

He nodded. "That's never easy. I know." A silence fell between us, but not an uncomfortable one.

Wait. How did he know? "This has happened to you?" I asked.

After a moment's hesitation, he said, "It was a long time ago. I try not to think about it. That's not why you're here, though."

"True. Do you want to have lunch?" I asked as innocently as possible.

"Lose the look. I know you want to ask me questions. Don't get involved. This has nothing to do with you." A hardened expression clouded his face.

"What about my brother? Does it have anything to do with him?"

"Listen. To. Me." Oliver punctuated each word with a tap on the desk. "Unless you've something to add or share or tell me—not show me, not investigate, not speculate—*tell* me, we're not discussing homicides or missing persons."

If that's how he wanted to be, fine. "No worries. The last time we talked, you were kind enough to check in on me." I stood. "I see that has changed. Goodbye."

Oliver groaned loud enough to be heard the next building over. "Ava, wait."

I kept my back to him. "I'm tired of men deciding what I need to know or when I need to know it. If you don't have something to say to me, fine. If you do, say it. You're not my friend if you want to play information games."

"Information games?" he asked, amusement lacing his voice. His chair squeaked.

I shrugged, fed up. I didn't want him thinking I only wanted to have lunch with him to learn what he knew about Quinn and Shaman Joe. While partially true, I also cared about Oliver. As a friend. I whirled around to face him. "I'm going to ask about my brother, Oliver. I'm going to want information. I was there, remember? It'd be weird if I didn't say anything. You texted me when I was in Stonington and asked if I wanted to get together, remember? We never had a chance to do that, so I thought I'd ask now. It just so happens that other things are going on simultaneously. If I ask you a question, you don't have to answer. In fact, you usually don't answer. So do you want to have lunch or not?"

He smiled the first genuine smile I'd seen on him in a while. "I guess you told me. Yes to lunch." The smile disappeared as he gathered the papers on his desk, tapping them into alignment. "But first I have a question. You've met Tory and Stanley's family. Did you happen to overhear any conversations while you were there? Did Tory or her boyfriend say anything about birds? Or wings?"

"Stanley's dad is all about birds. The first morning I was there, he was up early and looking at birds in the backyard. And I know he's here for the conference about birds. Or something like that." I should've paid more attention. "All I know for sure is that Stanley worries he won't recognize bird species when they fly overhead."

"Did anybody in that house, especially Valdorn, talk about a queen? Or someone named Alexandra?"

I tried to remember. "I'd met Sydney, so I was a little preoccupied and not listening to their conversations. Who is Alexandra?" Could she be connected to Shaman Joe? Or Quinn's death? Perhaps a love triangle?

"It's part of what we're trying to trace," Oliver said.

I took my phone out and added Queen Alexandra to my notes.

Oliver narrowed his eyes. "What are you doing with your phone?"

"Nothing. Meet me at the coffee shop?" I asked. "Lunch?"

"Sure, great. Around one o'clock?" He picked up a pen, poised to write.

"I'll be there. And Oliver, since I'm dealing with this Sydney thing and men dating inappropriate women… who are you dating right now?" Not my most delicate line of questioning, but I couldn't wait. Curiosity was my downfall.

He scrunched up his face, a new look for him. "Nobody. What kind of question is that?"

I shrugged. "Who do you still care about?" Maybe if I reworded the question, I'd get the answer I was looking for.

He twirled the pen he'd been holding. "Again, nobody. What's this about?"

"I thought you—I heard that you were—nobody?"

"Nobody. Now get out of here so I can get some work done. I've got a lunch date I need to be on time for."

Date? That was just a figure of speech, right? Anyway, it was clear he wasn't going to answer any more questions.

If I truly planned on becoming a private investigator, I needed to get real-world experience. I couldn't legally accept Chase's offer of payment to find Valdorn because I wasn't licensed to do so. Still, an informal investigation might help me make a final decision about my potential career path. One way to find out if I'd be any good at this would be to start poking around in what was going on, right?

Maybe not. Do I want to carry a gun? Do I want to get involved in everyone's drama? How many dead people can one person find in their lifetime? Maybe I should get another job at a library and keep my life sane. But that hadn't worked out too well the first time. I hated being indecisive. Whatever my path, I needed to decide soon.

I had some time before I met Oliver, time enough for a trip to the library to look up… I checked my phone. Queen Alexandra. The gentle strum of my ringtone interrupted my thoughts. The caller ID read Stanley. My finger hovered over the button. *To answer or not to answer.* I wondered if he knew about his father's visit to my apartment. That would be an interesting conversation.

I pushed the green button. "Yes?" A curt attitude worked best. I didn't want Stanley to get the wrong idea and think he could march back into my life.

"I miss you."

My heart melted. Then I thought of Sydney. I straightened my back. "If you say so."

"Are you busy?"

"No. Yes. Maybe." I could've kicked myself.

"Come over for coffee or tea or something. Let's talk. Please."

"There's nothing to talk about."

"I can come to you. You said you had one of my books."

The last thing I wanted was to have Stanley in my house. "I'll bring you your book, but that's it. We're done. I mean it."

"When should I expect you?"

"I'll drop it off right now." So much for going to the library. I'd stop by my house, grab the book, and walk around the corner to Stanley. This shouldn't take too long.

I sped back to my house, ran up the stairs, and grabbed the book off the end table. I didn't want to drag this thing out. I didn't stop for anything. By the time I arrived at Stanley's, I was out of breath.

He answered the door, surprised. "That was fast."

I held the book out to him. "Here you go. Thanks for letting me read it." I hadn't had a chance to read it, but he didn't need to know that.

He opened the door wide. "Come in." Seeing my reluctance, he added, "Please."

"I don't think that's a good idea."

"Five minutes. I won't take any more of your time, I promise."

I thought about it. Stanley had been there when I almost got killed. He was there when I landed in the hospital. I could spend five minutes with the guy. "Four would be better," I replied. I stepped past him and marched into the kitchen. I'd brew a quick cup of coffee on his Keurig. That should occupy me for the five minutes. I selected a French brew pod and loaded it into the machine. Stanley came behind me and put his hands on my shoulders. "I don't want to lose you. I love you, Ava."

I shrugged his hands off and stormed to the refrigerator, where I knew he kept flavored creamer for me. "You have a choice, Stanley. You lose me, or you lose Sydney. You can't have us both." I poured the creamer into my coffee, took a spoon from the drawer, and stirred. "I'm not sure why you thought you could date me when you never resolved your last relationship."

Stanley rubbed the back of his neck. "I know. I should've talked to her. And you. I know I need to figure out what to do with her. I care about her. I always will. But the first time I saw you, I wanted to get to know you better." He met my gaze, eyes filled with tears, and reached for my hand. I stepped away as he kept talking. "The longer I live here in Brewster Square, the more my life in Stonington seems like another world. I should've told you about Sydney, but I didn't want to lose you."

"And how did that work out for you? Your behavior isn't any better than your friend who was boffing Sydney." I sipped my coffee. "I mean it. If you want me in your life, Sydney's gone. Period."

The seconds ticked by. My throat closed, but I took a final swallow of the coffee anyway. I put the half-empty cup in the sink and turned back to Stanley. "Goodbye. Good luck with whatever your future holds."

I left Stanley in the kitchen and headed for the front door. The look on his face told me he wouldn't follow. I held my breath until I made it outside and reached the sidewalk.

That went well. Why does he think I'm going to sit around and wait for him to drag out his emotional drama with Sydney?

"I'm sorry my brother's an asshole." The voice behind me was emotionless. "He's always like that when it comes to her."

Surprised, I turned. I hadn't expected solidarity from Tory. "I had no idea she existed," I admitted. "I wouldn't have dated him if I'd known about her." I cringed at the idea of Tory thinking of me as "the other woman."

"They've been playing this game since they were teenagers. It's old and boring, and they need to get over it." She spread her fingers out, examining her black, paint-chipped nails. "You're not the worst he's brought home."

High praise indeed coming from an Elvira wannabe. I used the moment to my advantage. "Have you heard from Valdorn yet?"

She shot me a hostile look, and I stepped back. From friendly to murderous in under two seconds. I seemed to bring this out in some people. "No, but I'm not worried. He's with his old friends."

Valdorn had friends? Oliver hadn't said anything about friends. "Friends? Here?"

She sighed and folded her arms across her chest. "Yeah. He saw them at the conference, but he didn't want to tell anyone who they were." I flashed back to a conversation where Chase asked Valdorn about the people he'd been talking to. Valdorn had practically denied talking to anyone and only reluctantly admitted he "sort of" knew those guys. Tory kept talking.

"When he was a kid he got into some trouble, you know?" I didn't know, but I nodded. Anything to keep her talking. "Our criminal justice system—which totally sucks—sent him away. He was a kid. What the hell, right?"

For all I knew, he'd ripped the whiskers off baby opossums and deserved to get sent up the river. But I nodded. Tory didn't notice my ambivalence. Or didn't care. It was hard to tell. "He said the only reason he survived juvie was because of the friends he made in there. Said it was a place that killed your soul."

"What did he do?" I asked.

Tory shrugged. "I don't know, but he said it was nothing major, so whatever. They wanted to pin something on him, so they did."

I doubted he'd been a paragon of virtue as a kid. I needed to move this conversation along. "It's cool that he made friends in there," I said, grasping for something nice to say.

"Yeah, he was supposed to see his friends this weekend. That was the main reason he came here. They have something to do with this bird conference thing. Plus, they live here."

"Here?" I squeaked. Why the hell hadn't she said anything before?

Thoroughly bored with me, Tory sighed again for good measure. "Yes, that's what I said. They live near here. They have a condo over the coffee shop."

"Big Beans? I don't think I know anyone who lives there."

"Why would you? Val told me these guys are world travelers. They come from wealthy families. Like Val, they got caught up in a bogus charge and sent away as kids. Val said he thought it was because their parents couldn't handle them."

Somehow I doubted it was that simple, but stranger things had happened. "Who are they? I may know them from around town."

Tory looked up at the sky, thinking. A niggle of doubt eased down my spine. "He only talked about them a couple of times... some rich boy names… Pierce someone and Gavin someone else. Coates?" She directed her gaze at me and nodded. "That's it, Pierce Coates and Gavin Prescott. It's been real. Gotta go."

Chapter Twenty-Three

Valdorn's disappearance. Shaman Joe's disappearance. Quinn's murder. They had to be related, but I couldn't see the link between the three no matter how I flipped the puzzle.

I had an inkling Tory was setting me up. But why? Chase had been clear when he spoke to me that morning: do what you can to find Valdorn. Didn't Tory want the same thing? Why would she drop hints and walk away? Apparently, Stanley and his family had dark layers that I never would have thought possible.

I checked my phone and saw it was noon. I had an hour before I met Oliver for lunch. Tory wanted me to have a visit with Valdorn's delinquent friends. Their place was close to where Oliver and I were meeting. I thought through the potential risks of what I was about to do. Tory had sent me, though, so it couldn't be too dangerous.

I crossed the Green to Big Beans, the coffee shop owned by my friend Kenny. Kenny and I had known each other since elementary school when I punched him in the face for saying he wanted to kiss me. I'd made the mistake of dating him for a very short time in high school, a mistake I still regret. We'd remained friends, and Kenny had done well for himself.

I suspected his good fortune didn't come from purely legal means, but it was none of my business. Kenny and Giuseppe hated each other, their animosities exacerbated by the fact that Kenny had his own ghost-hunting business. The two were in constant competition.

Despite being owned by Kenny, who had zero sense of style, Big Beans was a cool, funky, and artistic kind of place, and along with serving a range of coffees and teas, they had simple, delicious food. My brother might not like Kenny, but I loved his food.

I paused in front of the building. The apartments over Big Beans probably had a separate entrance around the back. I walked to the back of the building. Nothing. I went to the front again and examined Big Beans and the neighboring buildings. Wait, there it was, a plain door off the entrance to the coffee shop. *I bet that's the stairs to the apartments.*

I opened the glass door and checked for buzzers. No buzzers, but a row of four small metal mailboxes were mounted to the wall. *Bingo. This must be it.* I climbed the steep steps, avoiding the railing. The narrow stairway had a musty, funky smell, as if piles of unwashed clothing were hidden somewhere, and the walls were full of dings and marks. At the top of the stairs, I inched down a short hallway with two doors on each side. My heart beat wildly, and I turned to leave. *What am I thinking? This is stupid.* I took a couple of steps down before my pulse shot back up. A shadow darted across the glass door and stopped. An indistinct figure cupped their hands around their face and peered in through the dirty glass.

I shivered and scampered upstairs to knock on doors. How bad could it be? I chose a door and knocked. After counting to thirty with no answer, I moved on to the second door. Before I raised my hand, the downstairs door squeaked open. *Someone's coming. Of course someone's coming, you idiot, people live here,* I chastised myself.

The apartment door opened to reveal a bored-looking, twenty-something-ish man with artfully tousled hair and a smug vibe. He wore khakis and a button-down shirt. "We don't want to buy anything."

"That's good because I don't want to sell anything," I said. "Are you Gavin Prescott?"

He straightened up, suddenly alert. "Listen, if this is about last weekend, I'm sorry. I should've called you, but I've been busy." He started to shut the door as I heard footsteps pounding up the stairs.

I pressed my palm on the door. "No, this is about a mutual friend. I'm here because of Tory." Hopefully the person coming up the stairs was a resident, not a killer.

A voice chimed behind me. "Tory's boyfriend, Valdorn, disappeared." Not a resident and definitely a killer, though she claimed she was better.

"Debbee, what brings you here?" I said through clenched teeth, hoping my frustration didn't show. I needed to act like everything was fine so this guy would talk to me.

She brightened as if all was right with the world. "Hey, friend! Trying to help. Friends don't let friends go into strangers' houses alone."

"Friends?" The word popped out before I could stop it.

"Who's at the door, man?" A Gavin look-alike appeared next to Gavin, with the same type of hair and clothing. "Dude. Is this about last weekend?"

They must've had a good time if they couldn't remember who they were with last weekend. I shook my head. "No. Like I said, I—"

"Why are you here then?"

"Tory told me you were friends with Valdorn. I'm trying to find him." I tried to get a look behind the Bobbsey Twins to see if Valdorn was in the apartment.

An amused look crossed their faces. "Would you like to come in?" the other one, who I assumed was Pierce, asked. He looked at his watch, which I noted was a Patek Philippe. "We wanted to catch the closing talks at the Ornithology Conference, but we have a little time."

I hesitated. No doubt they were connected to Valdorn, as that was the same conference Chase was in town to attend. Tory had said Valdorn went to the conference to catch up with these guys. My choice was clear: enter a strange home with two strange men or stand in the hall with a woman who had already tried to kill me. Not much of a choice. "I'll come in." I stepped into the apartment with Debbee on my heels. Shooting her a look, I said, "So nice of you, thanks."

"Yeah, nice," Debbee echoed. Her face contorted with what I guessed was supposed to be some sort of message for me but only made her appear goofy.

"What are you doing?" I whispered.

"Saving you," she whispered back.

The four of us stood in the center of the living room. My nose wrinkled at the smell. A mixture of unwashed laundry and the remnants of greasy food in wrappers scattered across the furniture contributed to the unique aroma. Debbee looked scared, like she knew something I didn't.

Both men threw themselves onto the couch, and Gavin pulled out a joint. *Seriously? He's going to—?* He lit it, inhaled deeply, and offered it to Pierce while Debbee and I hung out close to the door. Pierce ignored him, so Gavin motioned to us. We both shook our heads. I needed to get this interview back on track. "So, you know Valdorn?" I avoided mentioning jail time or juvie or criminal anything.

"Dudette, we met in jail," Gavin said. "He's helping—" His words were cut short by a scathing look from Pierce.

"Why are you interested in our friend?" Pierce asked.

I was distracted by a clicking noise coming from Debbee. She held a necklace made of cheap orange beads and moved them one at a time along the string. "What are you doing?" I asked in a low tone.

"Komboloi!" Gavin yelled. "I've got some too!" He jumped up from the couch and ran into another room, returning quickly with beads like Debbee's, except olive-colored. "Worry beads," he told me. While they bonded over talking bead strategy or whatever, I turned to Pierce.

"I met Valdorn at a family dinner with his girlfriend."

Pierce nodded. "The lovely Tory. But why are you here? You must admit, it's a little odd for you to show up at the home of two men you don't know to ask questions. What do you want with our friend?" He seemed genuinely puzzled.

Honesty was the only answer. "I'm trying to help her find him. He's missing."

"No he's not," Gavin said, interrupting his bead talk. "He sent us a text yesterday, said he was hiding out in that fleabag motel." He rubbed a bead back and forth. "Wait, why was he hiding?"

Someone should lay off the wacky tobacky, I thought, remembering what my father called it.

Pierce stood. He was sharper than Gavin, who was like a goofy puppy. Sharper, and more dangerous. "We can't help you. Perhaps it's time for you to go. Women shouldn't visit strange men."

The conversation wasn't working out the way I wanted it to. Someone banged on the door, and I jumped, then relaxed when I heard who it was. "This is your landlord. Let me in."

Pierce went to the door but didn't open it. "Do you have an appointment to enter the premises?"

The answer was swift. "I have an appointment to punch you in the nose if something happens to Ava."

Pierce opened the door to be greeted by my scowling ex, Kenny. "What the hell are you doing up here?" Kenny asked me, like it was my fault I was in danger.

"Following up on a lead. Besides, I'm fine," I said as I departed the apartment.

"You come up here all by yourself, and you think that's fine?" Kenny asked, outraged.

Debbee took this moment to speak. "She's not alone."

"You're the one who rented to these… dudes," I said.

"I'm right here. I came to help," Debbee repeated.

Kenny and I looked at Debbee. "You don't have the best track record," Kenny told her. "I wasn't sure who I was protecting her from."

"Oh, for God's sake," I huffed and stomped down the stairs. "I have to go. I have things to do." *Things* being trying to figure out which fleabag motel Valdorn was staying in so I could tell Tory and Chase. Then I could find Shaman Joe, and the police could figure out what happened to Quinn. Case closed.

Chapter Twenty-Four

Kenny followed me down the stairs and outside. We argued on the sidewalk while Debbee looked on with interest. Finally, I had enough and faced her. "Why are you staring at us? Don't you have something to do?"

Her eyes lit up. "Yes, I do, thank you." With that, she turned and strode away, barely waiting for traffic to let up before she crossed to the Green.

Crap. What is she up to?

"I don't like that," Kenny said. For once, I had to agree with him. "She's up to something. Why'd they let her out?"

I shrugged. "I have no idea. She said something about taking meds when she apologized."

Kenny nodded. "I hope she sticks with it. Mental illness is difficult to manage. She seems nice enough underneath her issues."

Kenny kept his eyes fixed on Debbee, who was now a speck in the distance. "Hey, don't forget she tried to kill me." I reminded him.

"Yeah, I know. But you put yourself in bad situations."

I gave up. This conversation was going nowhere. "I have to go. Goodbye, Kenny."

"Tell the aunts I said hello," he called.

I took ten steps before remembering where I needed to be.

"Now what are you doing?" Kenny asked as I brushed past him.

"Lunch," I snarled, hoping Oliver hadn't witnessed any of what just happened.

To my great relief, Oliver had no idea what I'd been up to. He didn't need to hear about Tory or my attempt to talk to the prep boys. At least not yet. I knew what he'd say, anyway.

He fidgeted in the seat across from me, frowning at his bowl of soup.

"Why are you eating soup on a warm spring day?" I asked.

He sighed. "I'm not hungry." He eyed my chicken cutlet and eggplant parm sandwich. It was large, but it was heaven. "That thing is huge."

I grinned. "I know." I picked it up, but Oliver continued to scrutinize me. I put it back on my plate. "I can't eat while you're staring at me."

"I'm waiting to see how the hell you'll fit that in your mouth."

When he put it like that, I wasn't sure I was hungry either. "Have you seen Debbee around town?"

He nodded and drank his coffee. Hot coffee and hot soup. Maybe he wasn't feeling well.

"She seems to be doing well. Is she bothering you?"

I couldn't answer that question without getting into the scenario that had happened upstairs, so I said, "Not really. You have anything fun planned this weekend?"

He snorted. "Trying to keep you safe and answering your pesky questions."

"Hey! I'm not pesky."

A smile tugged at the corner of his mouth. "If that's what you want to believe."

Our lunch was nothing more than a lot of gentle teasing and banter, but

Oliver seemed subdued. Again, I worried that he wasn't feeling well. Or maybe my guilty conscience saw problems where there were none.

"So there's nobody in your life right now? Nobody you might… care about?" I watched him for signs that he wasn't being truthful.

He raised his eyebrows. "Didn't you already ask me about this? I'm not dating anyone. I have no plans to begin dating or set up a Tinder app or anything like that." He took a sip of his coffee and carefully put it down. "Does this have something to do with Stanley?"

If he didn't want to talk, neither did I. "Nope. Do you watch baseball?"

He grinned. "Change the subject much?"

After an odd, low-key lunch, I said goodbye to Oliver and began counting steps as soon as I walked out the door. When I got home, I planned to look up New Haven hotels, but first I had to stop and see Aunt Maria. She'd tried to tell me something important about Sparky this morning. I got my dog and headed downstairs. Time to find out what she had to tell me.

I adored visiting with my aunts. They made me feel wrapped in love. They were thoughtful and took me seriously. The only problem with visiting was the food, as in, too much of it.

Aunt Sophia answered the door and gave me a big hug. "I've gotta go to the store. You be careful and behave," she called as she swung her purse onto her arm. "Maria's in the kitchen, go on back."

The kitchen, in the back of the apartment, always smelled wonderful. Older dark wood cabinets and a tan linoleum floor combined with more recent appliances to create a cozy space. I sat at the same kitchen table that had been there since I was a baby.

Aunt Maria put a piece of blueberry cake in front of me. Cake was her specialty; it'd be rude to say no to a slice of warm deliciousness. "What's going on with Stanley?" she asked.

My stomach flipped and I put my fork down. I hadn't expected the question. "Nothing. It's over. I'm done." Even my aunt's cake couldn't soothe my emotions. Sparky ran to me with a rubber ball attached to a rope, which I tugged while I pulled myself together. I had to tell my aunt what had happened.

It was one thing to be a strong woman and tell Stanley that I wasn't waiting around while he went back and forth between the ice goddess and me, but it was another thing altogether to put it into words for my family. I told my aunt about the trip to Stonington with my baby-puke hair, Stanley's family, Valdorn, Tory, the dinner, Charlie's engagement, Debbee's return, and Sydney. I talked nonstop for fifteen minutes, telling her about Shaman Joe and Quinn. The only thing I omitted was the shamanic experience at my brother's store. It was too weird to explain.

We sat for a moment in silence as Sparky continued to romp around the kitchen. Finally, Aunt Maria said, "That's a lot to handle all at once."

I met her eyes. "Stanley's behavior hurts, but it's better that I know now, right?"

My aunt cut another piece of cake and slid it toward me with a cup of coffee. "What about Oliver?"

"What about him?" I couldn't possibly eat another piece. I was still stuffed from lunch. The coffee, however, was great.

She sat across from me with her own cup of coffee. "He's not going to like that you're looking into this."

She was right. He'd be livid. "I know. I don't understand what G has to do with anything, though. He questioned him for hours the other night. My brother wasn't even around when Quinn was shot, so what's with all the questions?"

My aunt hesitated for a moment before answering. "Every investigation has aspects that law enforcement doesn't share with the public. Even though you have a friendship with Oliver, you're still a civilian. He's doing his job, and when he's able to talk about it, I'm sure he will."

The inquisitive side of me—okay, nosy—hated that answer. The practical side knew she was right. Sparky put his paws on my legs and dropped the tug toy on my lap. Somebody wanted to play. Again. "You said you wanted to talk about the dog." I gave Sparky the down command, which he obeyed but wasn't happy about. "Has he been bothering you? Did he eat a pair of your shoes or something?"

Aunt Maria sipped her coffee. "No, he isn't bothering anyone. We all love him; he's a delight." She paused, tucking a piece of her short blonde hair behind her ear, then added, "He's a special dog."

"I couldn't agree more." I looked at my canine friend, who, I swear, smiled at me. "He's a good boy."

My aunt continued to gaze at him with a thoughtful expression. "You might want to talk with others about this, but I have a feeling about your dog. Even though he's not a traditional breed for—"

Indignation rose fast. "There's nothing wrong with a mutt! He's perfect!"

"Yes, he is!" Aunt Maria agreed. "The thing is, with a dog like this, he has high energy. All he wants to do is play."

I nodded at the truth of that. The dog had a never-ending well of energy and liked nothing better than playing with a ball. Or a rope. Or a wadded-up piece of paper or a falling leaf or just about anything. "He's a sweetheart, isn't he?" I said, curious what my aunt was getting at about Sparky.

"I think your dog needs a job."

Great. Now I needed to find something for both of us to do with the rest of our lives.

Chapter Twenty-Five

The scent of garlic and tomatoes wrapped around me as I sat at my parents' farmhouse kitchen table. My mother proclaimed there were too many gnats outside, and we'd end up spending the entire dinner waving our arms in the air to keep them away, so we gathered in the large kitchen instead. I loved my mother's cooking as much as my aunts' cooking. We were a family blessed with fantastic cooks.

My parents lived on a farm in the farthest northwest corner of our town. My mother kept the house obsessively clean, adhering to the old adage "you could eat off the kitchen floor." Fortunately, that theory never got tested. Conversations washed over me as we spooned out portions of manicotti and passed around hunks of garlic bread. I put some salad on my plate, too. Mostly to look virtuous, as I didn't intend to eat it.

"Make sure you eat that," my brother said, nodding at my plate.

I feigned offense. "What do you mean? I love mom's manicotti."

"You know what I'm talking about. You need to balance your energy field with more greens."

I stuck my tongue out at him when he turned to help Baby Danny.

My father smiled and ducked his head, and my mother raised an eyebrow at me. Something about sitting around the dinner table with my brother brought out the kid in me. It happened to everyone, even the Queen of England. Or Madonna. Or RuPaul. I wondered, would—

"Ava!"

I jumped at my mother's voice. "Sorry, Mom. What did you say?"

"You were daydreaming again, like when you were a kid. I said, how have things been at the store for you? I noticed business has been brisk, but I wasn't sure if that was from the incident or if things have been busy in general."

My brother cut me off. "Business is good, Ma. Mercury is finally out of retrograde—" My father *hmphed* at that but didn't look up from his plate. Not for the first time, I wondered what my father thought about my brother's business of searching for the unexplained. "—but the one thing that's going to drive away business is those pesky salespeople."

"What salespeople, dear?" my mother asked.

Giuseppe broke off a piece of bread before answering. "They came in a few times and tried to sell me bugs." He gave a dramatic shiver. "You know, the kind that gets put in a little case after they're killed? They said it was a hot commodity right now."

Janine shook her head. "I remember you telling me about that. Gross is what I say. Who wants to buy a bug? What are people thinking?" She tore the bread into tiny bites and put it on Baby Danny's highchair tray, next to his cut up manicotti. She cooed at him, and he smiled back with a face full of pasta sauce. Janine struck me as not entirely on board with the whole organic food thing for the baby. Maybe she snuck him potato chips when my brother wasn't home. Or McDonald's Happy Meals.

"I'm glad I wasn't there to see the product," I said, pulling a hair scrunchie out of my pocket and putting my curls in a ponytail. "There's a market for that?"

Giuseppe shrugged. "I guess there is, but you'd think that kind of product would sell best at schools or to biology teachers. I said no as nicely as I could, but man, they're persistent."

I wondered what motivated people to go into the dead bug business. I couldn't imagine myself as a door-to-door bug salesperson. "What did this person look like? Did they look like someone who sells bugs?" I asked. There had to be some weird childhood trauma that pushed people to kill, mount, and sell insects. "And what kind of bugs were they selling?"

The topic of conversation hadn't put anyone off their food. My father had even gone back for seconds. Baby Danny smeared sauce across his face and his shirt. He chortled, telling us he loved his grandmother's food. And her food would probably stay down.

G gave one of his big, dramatic sighs. "I don't know what the bugs were. I simply told him to get out of my space with that kind of thing. But it was weird because it was two guys. Who needs two people to sell bugs? Two young and preppy guys, looking like they'd come from a class at Yale or something. Weird."

The manicotti felt heavy in my stomach. "Did you get their names?" I looked at my plate and tried to keep the worry out of my voice, but my mother glanced up sharply.

Giuseppe shook his head. "No, why? I got them out of the store as fast as I could. I didn't want any customers to see that. We specialize in things to quiet the soul and create an aura of peace, and those buffoons show up with little reminders of death."

My body grew cold. He was being facetious, but I had a feeling my brother's comment was more accurate than he realized.

I drove home without incident, a minor miracle given that I was thinking about bugs and preppy guys instead of watching the road. The motion-activated outdoor lights went on as I walked from the garage and around the side of the building. I always entered by the front door and never used the fire escape that ran up the building and led to the back door. The metal stairs made my footsteps extraordinarily loud, and I didn't entirely trust that it wouldn't separate from the building and come crashing down.

The beginning of a headache was starting behind my eyes, so I pulled the scrunchie out and shook my hair, not caring what it looked like at the moment. I had my key out and ready, on autopilot. *Maybe that shamanic vision thing was about Sparky. Maybe that's why I saw a dog. Pure imagination. But where the hell is Shaman Joe?* A train whistle jarred me from my thoughts, but it wasn't coming from a train. It was the new sound I had programmed as my ringtone. I initially thought it was a cool sound, but I second-guessed my decision as it echoed a plaintive cry through the dense night air.

"Are you busy?" Charlie's voice was a lifeline, anchoring me to the tangible reality of the here and now. I was safe, and there were no Lowerworlds or shamanic journeys or dead bugs in cases. There was just me walking into my secure apartment in the building I shared with my aunts.

"No, I'm home from dinner with my parents. What's up?"

"The wedding plans are coming together. We have a date and a place to get married. On June 5 of next year, I will officially become a married woman!"

I put the key into the lock and opened the front door. "That's great! Tell me everything." I walked up the stairs to the third floor, thrilled for my friend. She'd waited a long time for this wedding.

"We went with Chez Chez. It was available, and our wedding planner can get us a discount because of the amount of business she brings them."

Relieved to be home, I threw my keys into the bowl on the table next to my door, kicked off my shoes, and headed straight for the refrigerator. I needed a glass of wine tonight. "The food was good there, so that's what counts. What about music? Flowers? Colors?"

We chatted for another few minutes as she caught me up on her plans. It basically came down to string quartet, DJ, roses, and either teal or sapphire. Who said weddings were complicated? Charlie made it sound easy.

"What about you?" she asked. "Seeing another dead person? What's going on with the shaman man and Tory's weird boyfriend? And Stanley." She said the last words softly, knowing it was a sensitive subject in that instinctive friend way.

"I didn't know the guy who got killed, but Giuseppe said his name was Quinn. Finding another dead person wasn't fun, but I didn't have an emotional attachment to him." I stopped, my throat closing. *Like with Ethel*, I thought. I'd known Ethel for years, so it'd been difficult for me. Any violent death was brutal to look at, but at least I hadn't known Quinn.

"Ava?" Charlie's voice interrupted my thoughts. "How are you really?"

I took a breath. "Shaman Joe is still missing," I said, frustrated. "I'm worried about him. For all his weirdness, I liked him. He was sweet." I caught myself. *I'm talking about him in the past tense. I can't do that.* "Scary boyfriend is missing, and Stanley's dad wants me to find him."

"Win doesn't like Stanley's dad," Charlie said. "Normally everything Win says is to be taken with a grain of salt, but in this case, I'm not so sure. I heard him talking to you about Chase the other day, and a little later he pulled me aside and said to watch out for him. He seemed a little worried about you being with Stanley."

"That's a big change for Win," I said, thinking of all the times he'd tried to undermine Charlie.

Charlie gasped. "Right? See what I meant when I said he's got some terminal illness?"

I ran my hand through my hair, trying to dislodge a knot. "He doesn't have a terminal illness. He's had a life-changing experience and has seen the error of his ways. Kind of like seeing the ghost of Christmas past."

Charlie giggled. "He saw the ghost of Christmas future and he liked the look of his grandbabies."

I froze. "Charlie?"

"Yes?"

"Are you pregnant?"

"Not yet. But we're talking about it. We want to have children soon after we marry."

I imagined Charlie as a mom. "You're going to be awesome parents."

I'd finished a glass of wine by the time I hung up with Charlie. Instead of doing more research, I decided to go to bed. *After the events of the past few days, I should sleep well tonight.*

But sleep was uneasy and fitful. I tossed and turned with thoughts of Oliver and Queen Alexandra and bugs peppering my dreams, all mixed into a long dream that mirrored my shamanic journey.

Chapter Twenty-Six

As much as I wanted to dive right into research, I had to be at work Monday morning, especially after my mother had been in the store. She meant well; my brother and she didn't exactly agree on how to display merchandise. He organized items according to theme, and she shelved them according to size, from big to small. To his credit, my brother never reprimanded her; we simply reorganized after she left.

I'd slept later than usual. I fed Sparky, gulped down a cup of coffee, and off we went. Another sunny day, which was unusual for Connecticut. Where were the gray skies and drenching rains I knew so well? The scent of lilacs from the bush in front of my house wafted by as I counted steps to the store.

Giuseppe's scrunched-up face greeted me when I walked in, like he used to look when he was a kid doing his algebra homework. "Hey, G, what's happening? Did you lose something?"

"The numbers are off," he said.

"Like when you were a kid."

"Huh?"

I suppressed a giggle. "What numbers?"

"I'm missing some merchandise. I did a quick inventory while I restacked the stuff Mom moved, but it looks like either some sales didn't get rung up properly or, you know."

He hated thinking anyone might steal from his store. I admired his desire to believe in the best of people, but sometimes people didn't have the highest of intentions when they shopped.

"Here, I'll help. I'll put Sparky in the office first, and we can do this together." Once in the office, the dog sniffed every inch of the space. "Don't you dare," I whispered, thinking he might try to eat the papers or the desk or the walls. I'd have to take him out for a long walk on my lunch break.

I shut the door, twisted my hair into a knot, and joined Giuseppe. We started over, rearranging items and counting inventory, and in the end, the numbers worked. "Looks like everything is here."

"That's a relief. I must've gotten distracted while I was counting."

Once everything was back in place, I decided to question Giuseppe. He knew something that could point me in the right direction. "So, G, I wanted to ask you more about Shaman Joe."

"Don't call me G. What about him?" He had pulled out the recent issue of New Age magazine and flipped through the pages.

"He's still missing, and I'm trying to figure out what happened. I liked him. Can you tell me anything more about him?" I grabbed the duster and started cleaning the shelving area near my brother.

Giuseppe looked at the ceiling and sighed. "It feels like everyone has been asking me either about him or Quinn or bugs. Between the three things, I wish the police would focus on Joe."

"The police are asking you about bugs?" I was surprised. Why would they ask about that? I remembered Giuseppe's description of the two men who came in, and a sense of disquiet moved through me. I'd met two men matching that description, and I'd bet they never put their juvie days behind them despite what the justice system might think.

"It's weird," my brother continued, squinting at the magazine. "Your friend, Oliver, is all over the place with his questions. And I can't for the life of me figure out what he thinks I did wrong. I wasn't even there when Quinn died."

I didn't know either, but I didn't like it. Oliver wasn't telling me the details of this investigation. "You said you didn't know Quinn. Did you remember anything about him? Maybe something someone else said? He must have known you since he was here for the workshop." The shelving unit was completely dusted, but I didn't want to end the conversation so I started dusting the same thing.

Giuseppe hesitated. "I'd seen him around before, but he wasn't a regular. He traveled a lot. Whenever I saw him out somewhere, he seemed to flash a lot of money around."

I shook my head. "I don't remember seeing him before that night, but it's possible I just never noticed him. Where's he from?"

My brother scrunched up his face. "Hartford, I think? Some weird little town outside Hartford?"

"So… Joe? Do you have any insight?"

Giuseppe shook his head. "I already told you about Maya and Jacob."

I let the silence drag out. I'd read it encouraged people to talk more. The steady humming of the overhead lights filled the air, punctuated by the sound of magazine pages turning. Finally, I gave up. The method probably only worked on everyone who wasn't my brother.

"Did he have any hobbies?" I asked. Maybe Shaman Joe had left on his own and gone back to what was familiar in his life, whatever that might be.

Giuseppe looked up. "Who?"

Don't be annoyed, don't be annoyed, don't be— "Who were we just talking about?"

"I don't know," Giuseppe said. "We were talking, and I started reading, then you got quiet for so long I forgot what the heck you were asking."

I waved the duster in the air, shaking out everything I'd just picked up. "Shaman Joe?"

"That's right, hobbies. He used to do some kind of martial arts thing for fun."

"Martial arts thing? What does that mean?"

Giuseppe scrunched up his face again, which wasn't a good sign. "It was dancing?"

I bit back a sigh and wondered at the miracle that we had the same parents. "Are you asking me?"

He straightened and gave me a look. "Well, no, why would I ask you?"

"Because you said it with a question mark?"

"So did you just now."

This wasn't helping. I tried to get us back on track. After all, I could only pretend-dust for so long. "Okay, martial arts and dancing."

Giuseppe nodded. "It was some combination of the two things. Cap… a… capa…"

It clicked. "Capoeira," I said. "It's a Brazilian martial art with music and dance. I remember seeing a demonstration once. It's kind of cool." This was great information. I didn't think there were too many places where someone could practice Capoeira. I'd track down wherever he'd learned it and get some clues about him and where he might be. Easy peasy.

"Right, that's what it's called. He stopped doing that."

Well, crap.

"He started boxing instead," my brother said. "He liked straight-up fighting better than the Brazilian thing. Said it was more fun." Giuseppe put his magazine under the counter and started straightening the notecard display next to the register.

Not my definition of a good time. "Fun? Who fights for fun? And why do I sense that you think it's fun, too? What happened to my peace-loving brother?"

"It's a guy thing, I guess. You wouldn't understand."

He was saved from my scathing retort by the store phone ringing. Giuseppe moved to answer it, and after he did, he turned and faced me. "She's fine. Why?" His face paled. "What? Okay, hold on." He held the phone out for me wordlessly.

"What happened? Who is it?" *Please don't let it be our family*, I prayed.

"It's Stanley. You'd better talk to him."

I took the phone. "Stanley? What happened?"

"Ava, thank God you're there. I—I…"

Stanley mumbled something unintelligible, but I could hear his distress. I waited while he composed himself. "It's okay, whatever it is. You're okay. Take your time," I said.

"Valdorn is dead. They found him today."

It took my brain a moment to catch up with what he said. "Dead? How? What happened?" I imagined the dumbass had gotten into an accident of some type. I couldn't bear to think it was deliberate, no matter how much I hadn't liked the guy.

"He was murdered. Police found him in a hotel room in New Haven this morning. Ava, you need to be careful. Two people are dead. Something is going on, and you don't want to be part of it."

Chapter Twenty-Seven

I hadn't followed up on the hotel clue and now the guy was dead.

"Go," Giuseppe said. "It's a terrible death. You cannot possibly work today."

My eyes filled with tears. He was right. Another death was, to say the least, extremely unsettling. It was sweet of him to understand. "Mom would kill me if I made you work today," he added. My assumption was misplaced, but at least I could leave work.

"I'd better go to Stanley's house. I'll call you later." I went to the back to get Sparky.

"You can leave Sparky here. I have a feeling you'll be going to more places than Stanley's. And don't let that guy steamroll you, especially now that everyone's going to be all sad and crying and whatever."

I stared at my brother. "What do you mean?"

"He has that other woman hanging around, and you deserve to be treated better." He stood taller and glowered. "If you need me to talk to him, I will. He shouldn't treat you like that."

"Thanks, G." I hugged him. "I'll come by later to pick up Sparky. You're the best."

"Yeah, I know." He waved me away. "Go, do what you have to do."

It was awesome when my family understood me.

I opened the front door without knocking, balancing a basket of fruit in one hand while the scent of coffee and bacon drifted around me. I wanted to catch any bits of conversation before everyone clammed up on me, and I had the perfect excuse for showing up and entering unannounced: delivering sympathy food. Chase had asked me to find Tory's boyfriend, and I hadn't done it in time. I remembered Tory's suggestion that Valdorn was with his old friends. Was she looking to point suspicion at someone else for his death? Another part of me thought Stanley might know more than he was saying. But most importantly, I needed to find Shaman Joe. Both Valdorn's and Quinn's death highlighted that something dangerous was happening.

A good private detective would creep in with great stealth, overhear a meaningful conversation, and crack the case wide open. I wasn't a good detective. I wasn't even mediocre. I was so focused on ascertaining where everyone was, that I knocked over the oversized umbrella stand in the entryway.

This wasn't going well. Oversized umbrella stands make a lot of noise when knocked over, especially old and brass ones. It was heavy, too, and I dropped the fruit basket as I struggled to upright it. I hoped nothing got bruised.

When did Stanley get an umbrella stand? I didn't want to think about what it meant. As I fumbled with the mess, a shadow fell across me.

"What do you think you're doing?" Sydney sneered at me. "I'll have you know that's a family heirloom you're knocking around. Do be careful."

I abandoned my efforts and stood.

She looked down her nose at me. "Why are you skulking about?"

If Ms. Snooty-pants thought I'd simply whimper and go away, she had another think coming. "Oh, Stanley doesn't mind when I come in. He does the same at my place." I smiled. "You shouldn't put your furniture in the way. It'll get kicked over when I—when people come to the house."

Stanley appeared behind her, looking anxious. "Hey, Ava." He stepped over the fruit basket and brushed by Sydney so he could hug me. "I was so worried about you."

The petty part of me, the part I'm not proud of, smiled and hugged him back. "I'm fine," I murmured. "I came over to see how you and your sister are doing." And to find information, but I didn't say that aloud.

"And to see what we could tell her." Tory's nasal voice cut through the air. "You were supposed to find him."

I stepped back from Stanley. Tory hovered behind Sydney, who'd puffed up like a cat defending her territory. "I'm sorry for your loss," I said quietly. I was sorry. I thought of the poet, John Donne, who had written about being diminished by every death because he was part of the fabric of mankind. True, I wasn't fond of Valdorn. But I didn't want him to die.

Stanley cleared his throat. "This whole thing is bizarre. Do you want to stay for a minute?"

I looked from him to his sister, with her red-rimmed eyes and greasy, messy hair. My questions could wait. Despite my urge to torment Sydney, they didn't need me intruding on their grief. "I came to offer my condolences and give you this." I bent down, picked up the basket, and handed it to Stanley. "I'm sorry this happened."

Tory sniffed. "It's not your fault. This was bound to happen to him sooner or later. He shouldn't have been—"

"In the wrong place at the wrong time," Sydney interrupted. "Sometimes that happens when people go where they shouldn't."

Could she be more obvious as she glared at me? Yeesh. I glared back.

"Thank you for this," Stanley said, nodding at the fruit basket. "We appreciate your concern."

Sydney stepped forward and snaked an arm through his. "Yes, we do," she oozed. "This looks absolutely delightful."

Sydney played games because it's who she was. I had zero desire to interact with this trio of emotionally damaged people. "Take care of yourselves," I said, stepping away from them and turning to leave.

"Ava, wait," Stanley said.

I looked back at him. "You need to be with your family right now. We'll talk again." I still needed to gather more information, but this wasn't the time to question people. I might have wanted answers, but I didn't want answers at someone else's emotional expense.

I was exhausted after facing Sydney the barracuda. I stopped by the store, picked up Sparky, and went home. A little downtime and internet research was in order.

What makes a person so mean? Was she born like that, or did life grind the friendly right out of her? It was better to move on from Stanley and the toxicity hovering around him.

I sat at my computer, fingers poised above the keyboard. *What am I supposed to be looking up? Wait, I put it on my phone.* Queen Alexandra.

I typed the name in and read the results. The longest-serving Princess of Wales in British history. I doubted the princess was connected to anything. Aside from being long dead, she had nothing to do with Shaman Joe, Quinn, Valdorn, or the bugs Giuseppe talked about. *Unless her ghost is haunting someone.* I shoved the thought aside. I did *not*, repeat, I did *not* believe in ghosts. Probably not, at least.

I scrolled to the bottom of the search page. There it was: Queen Alexandra's Birdwing butterfly. A much better fit with the weirdness around me. I scrolled and discovered the butterflies lived in the rainforests of Papua New Guinea and were named for the Queen in England. In addition to being extremely rare, they were the largest butterflies on the planet.

I grabbed a piece of paper to make a list, hoping it would trigger an idea for me:

Quinn, plaid shirt, beard, dead
Shaman Joe missing
Chase and Valdorn here for bird conference
Valdorn missing around same time as Shaman Joe
Valdorn dead in hotel room
G approached to sell bugs
Oliver asked about Queen Alexandra

I sat back and thought about the last item. It was odd, that's for sure, and made stranger by the fact that those two clowns I visited were most likely the same dudes who approached my brother.

My phone rang, interrupting my thoughts. Aunt Maria. "Who is it?" I asked when I answered.

"Hot, hunky, and on the right side of the law." She laughed before hanging up.

I opened the door just as Oliver was about to knock, his hand still in midair. "That was fast," he said. "You must've had advanced intel I was coming upstairs."

"Nothing gets past my aunts. Come on in."

He walked in, all business. The way he carried himself told me he was on the job.

"Are you here in an official capacity?" I asked, knowing the answer.

His eyes narrowed. "Yes."

Chapter Twenty-Eight

I knew it." I led us into the kitchen. "Coffee? Tea? Are you hungry?"

"Would you please stop trying to feed me and sit to answer my questions?" He did say please, but that didn't soften his words. Sparky danced around his feet, hoping for a game of fetch or tug. Oliver patted him but otherwise stayed focused on me.

"Fine. Have a seat." I made a sweeping motion to indicate the counter chairs or the kitchen table, whichever he preferred. I continued standing for a slight advantage.

"I don't need to sit." Sparky gave a small yip, intent on playing with his friend. "Ava, what can you tell me about Valdorn?" He had pulled out a little notebook and started writing.

"Sparky, go to your bed." After the dog left the room, I turned my attention to Oliver. "I might not have liked him, but I'm not happy he's dead."

He shifted from one foot to the other, writing more on the small page. "Moving on. What do you know about Valdorn's past?"

I tried to organize my thoughts. "I know he was heavily into New Age-y stuff; I know he dated Stanley's sister Tory; I know he was connected to the guys above the coffee shop."

"Which guys? What are their names?" Oliver interrupted, looking up from his notebook.

I told him how Tory had fed me information and the story of Debbee following me around, how I ended up talking to the two frat boys, Gavin and Pierce, who lived over Big Beans, and my suspicion that they'd approached my brother about selling bugs. He nodded and looked down again, writing what I said. I kept the bug-selling judgment out of my voice but less so regarding Debbee. "She always knows where I am," I complained.

"As long as she takes her meds, she'll be fine. Tell me more about Chase and Tory."

Was I the only person worried about Ms. Crazy-pants? And why didn't he yell at me for talking to the prep boys?

I shoved the thought aside and launched into another long-winded explanation of what I knew about Stanley's family, including the fact that Tory had clearly set me up to find Valdorn. Oliver raised his eyebrows. "How did she set you up?"

"She told me about his friends and where they lived." As soon as I said it, I realized how lame it sounded. Maybe I simply didn't like Tory. Maybe she hadn't set me up. Oliver did not reply but continued writing. I ended with Win's comment. "I know Win is a stuck-up pain in the butt, but he seemed strident in his low opinion of Chase. I don't know what to make of that. On the surface, Chase seems like a nice enough person." I thought for a moment. "Then again, so did Stanley. I guess it's a family trait to be a jerk."

Oliver contemplated me and ran his hand over his face. "I'm going to tell you a few things, but you need to keep quiet about it."

I nodded and said nothing, demonstrating my ability to be quiet. I moved to the table and sat down, indicating the seat opposite me. After a moment, Oliver closed his notebook and sat too.

"Chase had a job as a university professor in New London."

"Wait, what do you mean 'had'?"

"I suppose he still has it, but that could change soon. He's currently on forced leave and is being investigated by the university. They aren't done yet, but we should know something soon."

"What did he do?" A horrible thought occurred to me. "Did he hurt anyone?"

Oliver shook his head. "It's more of a white-collar crime thing. He's not dangerous. But it hasn't been proven whether he did what he's accused of, so I don't want to say any more about it. But that might be why Win made that comment. He heard about this incident. Please don't repeat what I told you. As I said, the investigation isn't yet complete."

Whatever Chase had done, it'd be enough for Win to decide he wasn't someone to be associated with. I twirled a piece of my hair. "Anything else I should know?"

Oliver nodded, pulled out his phone, and showed me a photo. "This guy?"

I swallowed. "That's the dead guy. Quinn."

He put his phone down. "Yes. Quinn McCord. We have surprisingly little information on him. We know he traveled extensively, we know he kept large amounts of cash in his home, and we know he didn't have many friends or associates. You said you didn't know him, but have you heard anything about him since we last asked?"

"I wish I could tell you something that would help," I said. "But I never saw the guy before that night. My brother doesn't know him, either." I decided not to mention the small pieces that my brother had told me. It wouldn't help Oliver and it might make him drag my brother in for questioning again.

Oliver flipped his notebook over, then flipped it again before finally nodding. "We asked your brother. We asked everyone. We have no idea what this Quinn person was doing at your brother's store that night."

Shamanic journeying, what else? I wisely kept my mouth shut.

Oliver leaned toward me, serious. "I'm going to tell you something else that I don't want repeated."

I swallowed. He had his mean face on, which meant I shouldn't be a smart ass. "Okay," I croaked.

"The Brewster Square police department is working hard on this case." He stood suddenly, as if unable to contain himself any longer. "But there are also other agencies involved, working behind the scenes. You need to stay out of this, because these guys do not go easy on people who get in their way. Charges of obstruction are no joke."

He picked up his notebook, silent again. For a moment, the only sound was the ticking of my kitchen clock.

"Thank you for telling me," I said, heartened that he cared enough to share an obviously covert piece of information.

Since Oliver had stood again, Sparky grabbed his chance and belly-crawled closer to us despite his banishment to the dog bed. "Did you think I wouldn't see you?" I said to the dog. He rolled over, exposed his belly, and yipped. I tried not to smile, as I didn't want to encourage his behavior.

Oliver reached under the table and pulled out a tug toy. "Sparky, come." Sparky bounded over to Oliver, and the two played for a couple of minutes before Oliver let Sparky win the toy.

"Now go to your bed," I said in a firm voice. Tail wagging, he trotted back to his dog bed with the toy in his mouth. He flopped on his bed and played with his toy, alternately chewing on it and dropping and pouncing on it when it landed on the floor.

Oliver took his seat at the table with me and nodded at the dog. "How's he doing?"

"He's great. He likes to play. A lot. That dog can find a tennis ball hidden under a pile of anything. I don't know how he does it." I couldn't keep the pride out of my voice. "My aunt said he needs a job."

We sat, comfortably quiet, and watched Sparky play. "I know what he'd be perfect for," Oliver said, standing. "You, too."

This sounded intriguing. "What?"

"I'll get the information together and give it to you later."

"You can't say something like that and leave," I complained.

"Yes I can." Oliver smiled, radiating warmth. I smiled back, thinking how handsome he looked when he wasn't grilling me about crimes. "But you're right; that's not fair. I think you and Sparky would make a great team."

"Team?"

"Search and rescue. Every state operates differently. Most states have people who work with local law enforcement. Only a few states have statewide teams under their emergency management department. I'll talk to the folks who do it to see how they operate here and let you know what I find out."

I considered what he said. It sounded exciting, plus I'd get to have Sparky with me. "How much does a job like that pay?"

Oliver shook his head. "It doesn't, unless you're with law enforcement or the fire department. Most of the time it's a volunteer thing."

I remembered the volunteers who stood around outside my brother's store the night Shaman Joe went missing. "You're trying to get me to work for you for nothing?"

Oliver laughed outright, but his smile soon disappeared. "Ava, I've got to go, but please listen to me."

He's going to tell me to stay out of this.

"I need you to stay out of everything that's going on," he said.

That was an easy prediction. Now he's going to tell me—

"Ava, stop ignoring what I'm saying as if you know better."

I sobered. He was right. I wasn't listening to him because I thought I knew better. Isn't that what had happened last time? "Sorry," I said.

He leaned in close to me and spoke softly. "Do not go looking for Shaman Joe. People have died, and there may be more. I don't want you to be one of them."

Chapter Twenty-Nine

Search and rescue wasn't a paid job, but I could do volunteer work while pursuing a stable career. I wasn't drawn to fighting fires or policing because I didn't think my personality was a good match for that kind of work. But search and rescue dovetailed nicely with private investigation. I'd look into it later. Right now, I needed to find Shaman Joe, no matter what Oliver said.

I can do this safely. I'll stick to crowded areas and avoid being alone with anyone—my biggest mistake last time. I can't let Joe disappear or get killed without trying to help.

I sat at my desk in the alcove of my living room and thought about where to investigate. My brother had said that Shaman Joe liked to box, but he didn't say where. He also mentioned two people, Maya and Jacob. I dialed my brother's number and impatiently waited for him to answer.

"Yo."

Be nice. You want him to help you. "You busy?"

"What's up? You okay?"

"I'm fine. I had a few questions, though."

"Does Oliver know you're asking me questions?"

What the heck? "You don't even know what I'm going to ask you," I said.

"You're right. You wouldn't dream of asking me more questions about Joe, Quinn, or Valdorn."

"Valdorn's death is a police matter," I said stiffly. "I have nothing to do with that investigation." I fiddled with a pen, clicking it repeatedly.

"Glad you're staying out of trouble. Mom and Dad couldn't handle it if something happened to you."

I waited. "I wouldn't be too happy either," he added.

"Thank you. Geez. I wondered if you could give me Maya and Jacob's phone number." I figured he'd more likely give me a phone number than an address.

"I guess I can do that. You'll be safe calling them. Don't go off on your own trying to find Joe."

I looked at my dog lying at my feet. I wouldn't technically be alone if I brought Sparky. Plus, I'd stay near crowds. Hopefully. I wrote down the number and asked, "Are they connected to where Shaman Joe does his boxing thing?"

"Why?"

"Because I want to ask them about it." I sighed so he could hear me. He didn't need to know my real reason for asking, which was to track down the gym and find as much information as possible. Boxing was the only thing I knew about his past besides the shaman thing. I didn't want to investigate the shaman thing.

"I don't know. Maybe. He spends so much time traveling to South America that I don't even know how much time he has for the boxing gym anymore. Plus, he has an apartment in Arizona or New Mexico or something. Somewhere out there."

This was news to me. "Do you think he went home?"

"I don't think he's the kind of person who'd leave and not tell us." Giuseppe's voice held a note of concern that I shared.

The clip on my pen broke off and flew across the desk. Served me right for playing with it. "I think you're right. Thanks for the number."

"Don't do anything stupid."

"I can't believe you feel the need to say that to me." I hung up and hunched over my computer, about to do something stupid.

The drive to New Haven took all my concentration, and fortunately, Sparky remained curled up on the back seat and didn't distract me. The sun was bright, and it was another beautiful spring day. Despite wanting rain, I was glad for the warm weather. I hated driving on the highway in the winter when patches of ice wreaked havoc for people who were speeding. I worried I'd be in the way when someone lost control of their car.

The voice from my app told me where to go. *Turn left, and your destination will be on the right.* I was delighted when I saw several open spots for on-street parking, a major score anywhere in New Haven.

As soon as I'd ended the conversation with my brother, I entered the phone number into a data collection site I subscribed to. It provided detailed information about people, including addresses and criminal history. The search results showed the phone belonged to Maya and listed her address.

Easy peasy. Giuseppe didn't need to worry about a thing.

I put the car in park, snapped a leash on Sparky, and looked up at the house we were visiting. The two-story yellow Cape Cod had a red shingled roof. A cheerful row of red and yellow tulips bordered the front of the home, and the driveway looked newly paved. As I exited the car, my phone rang.

"Are you there yet?" my brother asked when I answered.

How the hell did he know where I was? "What do you mean?"

"I'm sure you did a reverse lookup thing and went straight to Maya and Jacob's house. Right?"

My brother knew me too well. At least he couldn't see my childish eye roll.

"I called and told them you're my sister and that you might be coming over."

"Why would you do that?" I demanded. He'd taken away my element of surprise.

"Because I didn't want you to scare them. I needed to make sure they knew you weren't some psycho trying to hurt people."

"They wouldn't think that. I don't even look scary. Neither does my dog."

"You're going to barge in there and start asking questions about a missing person. You're not with law enforcement, so they have no reason to talk to you."

He had a point. "Thanks," I said grudgingly.

"They were home just now when I called. Are you at the yellow house?"

I assessed the house in front of me. "It's adorable. I love the roof. And the windows—"

"This isn't one of those *Make It Pretty* home shows you like to watch," he interrupted. "Go in there, ask your questions, and go home."

"I was simply commenting on the aesthetics of the house. Yeesh."

"Go home after this."

"Thank you for your help," I said, ignoring his directive. I disconnected, and Sparky and I bounded up the sidewalk. The wooden front door had a curved top with a black iron knocker. Doorbell or knocker? I tried the knocker first. It creaked as I lifted it. A shadowy movement behind the front window curtains caught my eye as someone walked by.

I counted to twenty after knocking, and when nobody came to the door, I pressed the bell. I didn't want to pound on their door. I thought I heard shuffling inside. Maybe they were hurt or in trouble. After all, Giuseppe had spoken with them. I counted to ten and wiggled the door handle. Locked.

I rang the bell one more time. They weren't going to answer. Why, or what, were they hiding?

Chapter Thirty

Who knew there was more than one boxing gym in the immediate vicinity? How many people could enjoy hitting each other?

I didn't have any other leads to follow up on, and despite knowing that this might be a futile effort, I had to try to find out what I could. Maybe someone who had known Shaman Joe would know of other friends he had or places he might be hiding. It was a long shot, but I had nothing else to go on.

I was hot and tired after visiting two gyms to see if anyone knew Shaman Joe. The first gym was in East Haven, which I knew was probably not where he'd gone, but I checked out anyway. The other was on the outskirts of New Haven, where people worked out in fancy workout clothes. Both were a bust.

Now I was in the not-so-good part of New Haven, and after parking crookedly next to a fire hydrant (they could still get to it, I reasoned), I stomped down the street and tried to come up with another plan if this didn't pan out. Shaman Joe needed to be found, Sydney needed to go home, and Stanley needed to take a flying leap. I wasn't in a good mood. At least Sparky was enjoying himself.

Someone was following me. Frustration bubbled to the surface. I gripped Sparky's leash and spun around, ready to confront my would-be attacker.

Debbee jumped a little and waved. "Hi?"

"What the hell are you doing?" I shouted. A few people turned to look at us.

"I was just… there's a…"

"Stop following me! We don't have anything to say to each other." I pointed to the street. "You should go home."

She looked confused. "But I don't…"

"Just. Leave. Me. Alone." I said through gritted teeth. Without waiting for an answer, I resumed my search for the gym. There was no way she'd try to do something terrible to me in the middle of the street with everyone watching. At least, I hoped not.

I slowed my steps. Was it possible Debbee had something to do with Shaman Joe's disappearance? Why would she want to hurt a shaman? Crazy people didn't always make sense, but that truly made no sense. She liked Shaman Joe and there was no reason for her to hurt him. I had to admit that she had been looking out for me when we went up to Pierce and Gavin's apartment. *But following me is weird. When I'm not so cranky, I'll find out what she's up to.*

Spray-painted letters on the side of a building up the street read Gym, with no business name, along with a host of other artistic endeavors I chose to ignore. The brick was faded to a rusty brown, and pieces had crumbled off the top of the building. The rectangle-shaped structure had no decorative features.

I pushed open the glass front door, which looked like it hadn't been cleaned in eons, and stepped into a room ripe with the smell of sweat. A few young people punched heavy bags hanging from the ceiling, while others pummeled some speed bags. A few sullen teenagers lifted weights, and the ring in the center was empty. Everyone uniformly ignored me.

Fine. I'm not here to make friends. But you'd think they'd at least say something about Sparky.

Despite the warm day, I shivered. I needed information so I could get out of this place, but which of these disinterested jerks would talk to me? I approached the kid closest to me who was bench pressing something heavy. I waited until he put the weights down, not wanting to be responsible if he crushed his windpipe. "Excuse me, can you help me?"

He sat up and wiped his face with a towel from the floor. "Nope."

"But I need to—"

"I said nope." He stood and walked to another machine.

"You don't even know what I wanted. That's rude!" I yelled without thinking. Where were his manners?

Everyone stopped what they were doing. The gym got quiet. It wasn't going well. Where was crazy Debbee when I needed a distraction?

"What the hell is going on out here?" A large, bald man with a tank top over his muscular chest came out of a back office I'd missed seeing. "What are you all sitting around for? Get to work. This is no place for sissies."

He turned his piercing gaze on me. Nodding in my direction, he said, "Are you and your dog lost? We don't do dog fighting in here."

I held my anger. Dog fighting? Why would he think I wanted to do such a despicable thing? "I'm not lost, and we don't do dog fighting either. But it looks like the people in here are lost."

He balked. "What?"

"Lost as in they cannot remember their manners. Lost as in is this how you treat people who come into your place of business?"

He held up his hands in a gesture of surrender. "Okay, lady, sorry. They're kids, and they don't trust strangers."

One of the kids from a nearby weight machine piped up. "And you're definitely a stranger."

I glared at the kid, then realized he was right. "I guess I am."

Emboldened by my statement, he added, "And you ain't here to box."

"Are not," I said.

He shook his head. "Yeah, that's what I said."

Some of the kids hadn't gone back to working out. They fixated on Sparky pulling his leash, hoping to play. Trying to ignore the attention, I addressed Mr. Muscle. "Can I ask you something?"

He smirked. "You just did. But go ahead."

I pressed on, determined to ask my questions and go home. "A few nights ago, I was at a workshop at my brother's store. During the break, the teacher was beaten and left for dead out back, and someone else was shot. I'm sort of looking into what happened to the teacher who disappeared."

"Yo, someone died? You need protection?" The voice came from one of the kids who'd stopped punching the speed bag. "I can help. It'll cost you."

"Shut up, Billy," Mr. Muscle yelled before answering me. "Who is this teacher, and why do you think we know anything?"

He asked a legitimate question, and I wasn't inclined to play games or make anything up. These guys might turn scary. "I was introduced to him as Shaman Joe," I said, wondering if he had used any other names. "My brother said he used to spend time at a boxing gym, so I thought I'd check and see if you knew him. You're the last place on my list."

Mr. Muscle studied me for a moment. "What makes you so interested? You with the police?"

A voice came from the back of the gym. "Aw, man, she ain't with no police." Everyone around nodded their heads in agreement. Someone snickered. Sparky's ears went up.

I stared at the back of the gym, trying to see the kid who'd spoken, unsure whether I'd been insulted. "You're correct. I *am not* with the police. *Ain't* isn't a word. Besides, what makes you sure I'm not with the police?"

Mr. Muscle hid his laugh, but the kids didn't bother to try. "Maybe the grammar police," he said.

I stood straighter, trying to look tough. "A man died, and another was seriously hurt. He might be dead, too, although I hope not. Don't you want to help?"

It got quiet again. "Are you for real?" someone said.

"Of course I'm for real." My reasoning was outside anything these kids were familiar with. Sometimes my reasoning was outside anything anyone was familiar with.

"You should check with the police. I don't think we can help you."

"Can't or won't?" I challenged. I was hot and tired, and I didn't know where to look after this. Their belligerent attitudes made me wonder what they knew. And if they didn't know anything concrete, all I wanted from these people was some sort of direction, some clue where I could look next.

"Ava, it's okay." The unexpected voice came from my left. I turned and stared, blinking. Shaman Joe stood in front of me. "You can stop looking for me. I'm fine."

CHAPTER THIRTY-ONE

His face bore some bruises, but overall, Shaman Joe was alive. Unless I was seeing a ghost again.

"I'm alive," he said with a weak smile. "Let's go to the office and talk."

I threw my arms around him and gave him the gentlest of hugs. Sparky sniffed his pants. I opened my mouth to speak but couldn't. The last time I'd seen him, Quinn was lying dead next to him, then he disappeared, and now here he was hanging out in a gym.

"No need for tears," he whispered, returning my hug. "I'm fine." He bent over and petted Sparky, who remained calm for once.

I stepped back. "You're not just saying that?"

He shook his head and started to speak, but Mr. Muscle interrupted. "Joe, we need to go to the back office, like you said. I don't want anyone seeing you."

"Who's going to see him?" I asked, but nobody answered me. Instead, the men started walking. "It's not like they can see inside here," I continued. "You never clean the glass on your front door." A few of the young guys in the gym shook their heads. "It's true," I insisted. "There's smears all over that thing."

"Lady, seriously?" one of them said.

Instead of answering, I hurried to catch up to Joe and Mr. Muscle, Sparky trotting next to me. Mr. Muscle opened a gray metal door, and we all trooped in. An old, scarred desk and two rickety folding chairs furnished the room. It smelled like the rest of the gym: sweaty with an undercurrent of old food. I looked at the cinderblock walls, empty of anything except some water stains. Mr. Muscle must've never considered the psychology of decorating. A closed door was to my right, and I wondered if it led to the outside.

"You need to go?" Mr. Muscle asked.

"I just got here." Was he trying to kick me out?

He looked as if he were trying to hold on to his patience. "To the bathroom."

"Oh, that's where the door leads. No. Thank you."

I focused on Joe and the faint bruising on his face. "You look healed, but did anyone look at your injuries? What happened? Why are you here? Everyone's been searching for you. They had dogs at the store that night to see if they could find you, but they couldn't even send the dogs out." Something else occurred to me. "Was it Debbee? Did she hurt you? Because she can be—"

"It wasn't Debbee," he assured me. "It wasn't anyone you know. I'm sorry you had to witness that." He hesitated before speaking again. "It's best for you to remain in the dark about what happened. To some extent, I'm not entirely certain of all the specifics anyway."

I huffed. "You don't know why someone hurt you? That's going to complicate things. I don't have any working theories yet. How did you get away that night? I found you and," I paused. The memory of him lying back there made me feel helpless again. "You were pretty banged up. And Quinn died next to you."

Joe nodded. "Yeah, that was awful. I didn't know Quinn well, but I thought he was trying to turn his life around." He looked over my shoulder at some distant point. "I thought that since he'd shown up for the class, he was reaching out, making changes. He'd been holding in so much anger."

"Who did this to you? How did you get away?"

Joe pulled himself back to the present. "I suppose you have a right to know some of this after what you've been through." There wasn't much room in the tiny office, especially with Mr. Muscle standing there, so Joe did a half turn then faced me again. I noticed beads of sweat along his forehead. "I couldn't see their faces because they wore masks, but I think I know who it was. They've been after me to do something for them awhile." He studied his fingers. "I was shocked when I saw Quinn. I had no idea what was going on, only that Quinn was on the ground, bleeding. They came after me. After they beat me, someone opened the back door, and a dog started barking." He smiled at Sparky. "It scared them off. I managed to pull my phone out and text my friend Eric." He nodded at Mr. Muscle. "I crawled away and met Eric a little farther down the street. He picked me up and brought me here. The people who tried to kill me that night meant business. I couldn't stick around, especially after what they did to Quinn."

"Do you think they meant to kill you too?" I couldn't help asking. "How come—" I didn't know how to ask my next question without sounding harsh.

Joe gave me a sad smile. "How come they killed Quinn and not me? Quinn was already dead when I got out there. I didn't see it happen. But if it's who I think it is, they wanted something from me, so it wouldn't have made sense to kill me, too. And whoever came outside that night with their dog saved my life."

I squirmed, realizing that I had missed the killers by moments. "Do you know what they wanted?"

Joe paced in a small circle, as if he had to move, even within that tiny space. Mr. Muscle sat behind the desk. "They wanted to take trips with me and be introduced to the indigenous guides I work with. But I told them no, I work alone. Shamanic work isn't for everyone, and they didn't have the right attitude." He shrugged. "They didn't much like that answer."

I didn't much like any of this. "They can't exactly force you to take them with you. Where do you go?"

He hesitated before answering. "South America, usually. Sometimes Mexico."

I thought of Oliver and wondered if this had anything to do with his missing wife. "Is this about drugs?"

He shook his head. "It couldn't be. I don't use drugs, never take them, and I wouldn't know how to get any in those countries."

It was getting warm in that small office. I pulled my hair off my neck for a moment. "Do you think they're coming back?"

Joe nodded. "Yes, I have a feeling it's not over." He hesitated again. "I can tell you that they're ruthless. I've given this a lot of thought, and I think they are trafficking something or someone. My shamanic journeys tell me it might be animals, but I can't be sure." He sat on the edge of the desk, dislodging some papers. "If they think I'm useless, they won't hesitate to kill me too. That's why I've got to stay here until the police figure it out."

"But you're a witness," I argued.

"A witness the police will try to blame," he countered.

"They can protect you," I offered. "I can talk to Oliver if you want. Besides, you seem to know what this is about."

Joe's smile was weak. "That's kind of you to offer, but I'm only guessing. They were vague, and I can't always rely on visions. I am fairly certain they did not want me to know what they were doing." It made sense in a twisted way: the fewer people who knew, the less chance of getting caught. "The police deal with specifics, and how little I know doesn't usually work for them. They deal with the concrete aspect of being here on Earth. I'm a shaman, and I work with visions. Police don't like to hear about anything in the ethereal realm. Plus, after what happened with Valdorn, I'm afraid they're going to try to pin that on me."

"You mean his death? How did you hear about that?"

Joe shrugged. "He didn't die. He was murdered, like Quinn," he said. "It was all over the news."

I couldn't imagine Joe relaxing in front of the television to watch the six o'clock news or sitting down with a hot dog and beer to catch some TV shows. Maybe he'd read it in the newspaper over a cup of coffee. "But you don't know anything about Valdorn's death?" Part of me had hoped that I'd get answers to my questions by finding Joe.

"I'm afraid my guess would only implicate me more." He peered deeply into my eyes, which should've been uncomfortable but wasn't. "I didn't kill anyone, Ava."

"I believe you," I said without hesitation. I did believe him. I'd only met two people intent on killing others, and both times I'd had a weird feeling around those people. I still felt warm and safe around Joe. He was hiding something, but he wasn't a murderer. Still, I couldn't give up. Valdorn was an idiot, but he deserved to live out his life. I didn't know Quinn, but he deserved the same. "You might know something important that could help. Is there anything you can tell me? I'm not the police but I might be able to help."

Joe looked at the ceiling as if the answers were up there. "Everything's boiling over because of that birding conference at the college." He shook his head and stood from sitting on the edge of the desk. "Ava, I don't want to get you into trouble. Please, you have a gift. At this point, you should rely on that more than anything."

My neck prickled. Good God, he couldn't mean what I thought he meant. "Gift? You mean like the thing we did at your workshop?"

"Yes, and more. I know you deny it, but I also know you're able to see things from other realms."

I shook my head. "Nope. I don't believe in ghosts."

Both Joe and Mr. Muscle laughed, and Mr. Muscle said, "They believe in you."

I glared at him. What did he know, anyway?

"Use your gift to help you," Joe said. "Try not to ask too many questions of people who can hurt you. This will keep you safe. What you learn can guide law enforcement."

This kind of talk was making me squirm. But Joe was safe, and that was what mattered. I'd at least discovered one thing today. "Listen, I've got to go. Don't worry about me. I'm glad you're alive." I pointed at Mr. Muscle. "He's safe here, right? You're not going to let anything happen to him?"

Mr. Muscle held his hands up. "What, and have you march in here and harass us? Yes, ma'am, I'll keep him safe."

"Don't take that attitude with me," I snapped. "This is serious."

He sobered. "Yes, it is. He's safe. I promise."

"I have to go." I whirled to leave and called over my shoulder, "But I'll be in touch to make sure you're alright."

I didn't wait for a reply. Sparky and I marched out of the office and through the gym. Nobody paid any attention to us, which was perfect. I pushed the door open, kept my head down, and walked directly into a hard, solid body.

"Oof." I looked up, dazed, ready to offer an apology to whomever I'd walked into. My words died on my lips as I gazed into a pair of cold eyes.

"We should have some lunch," he said.

Chapter Thirty-Two

I liked diners. The predictability of the menus, the comfort food at a fair price, even the fake leather booths and wobbly tables charmed me. However, I didn't like when the person sitting across from me glared at me.

Oliver and I hadn't said a word since he'd grabbed my arm and marched me to my car. We'd stopped by my apartment building first to drop off Sparky with Aunt Maria, who had the good sense not to ask any questions when she saw the look on Oliver's face.

We gave our orders to the waitress who'd seen it all and wasn't the least bit interested in why her newest table sat as quiet as a tomb. I was torn between fear of his reaction (he could, after all, arrest me) and indignation at being treated in such a manner.

Indignation won. "Why were you following me?"

He gazed beyond me, toward the door, as if I wasn't even there. "Believe it or not, the world doesn't revolve around you. I wasn't following you. I was following a lead."

That, at least, made sense. But his attitude left something to be desired. "You could at least try to be nice to me."

He grunted and closed his eyes. "It's hard to be nice when I'm mad."

I grabbed my water glass then changed my mind. "What else is new? You're always mad."

His eyes narrowed. "What did you say?"

"I said you're always mad." The waitress set our food in front of us. Burger and fries for him, Caesar salad for me. I unrolled my napkin, pulled the fork out, and poked at a crouton. "You're always barking orders at me, and then you get mad." I didn't even try to stop the petulance creeping into my voice.

He exhaled loudly. "You're not the first person to say that to me."

Sadness and resignation crossed his face. I wondered if his wife used to say that to him. The silence stretched out a minute longer. It was time to change course.

I cleared my throat. "So. Search and rescue. Do I have to run into a burning building?"

Oliver tried to hide a smile. "No, that's a firefighter's job. You'd be working with law enforcement to find missing persons."

I remembered the dogs at my brother's store who didn't go looking for Joe. "But not all missing persons?"

"Correct," Oliver said. "It depends on several factors." He resigned himself to the change in conversation. "Typically, you and Sparky work together as a team with law enforcement. You'll go through training first. Every weekend you and your dog will work on topics like land navigation and rescue techniques. Sparky's a quick learner, but he'll need positive reinforcement and have to pass some tests. It's a lot of work, but it's worth it. You two will be great."

He reached into his pocket and pulled out a business card. "I talked to the head of the team; here's his number. Give him a call and ask about training. Tell him I spoke to you."

I took the card and read it: Connecticut Shoreline Search and Rescue,

CSSAR, and the name Reggie Dayton. "I don't know anything about rescuing people."

"They'll teach you. Besides, I have a feeling you've already learned a little about searching for people."

Another silence came between us while Oliver waited for a response. Finally, he said, "Did you find him?"

I froze, uncertain what to say. Was I in trouble? Was Joe in trouble?

"I was going into that gym when you came out," he said. I was torn. Joe needed help, but should I rat him out? I didn't know what to do.

Oliver sighed again, something he did a lot around me. "Not answering is an answer, you know. I've done a background on Joe. He's a good guy, never been in trouble. He's caught up in more than he can handle, though. Tell him to stay put while we figure this out. He's in danger."

Did he say we?

As if I had spoken out loud, he added, "And by 'we,' I don't mean you. You stay far away from this whole mess. Because it's a mess, and it's dangerous."

I nodded without saying anything. If he was going to keep harping at me to stay out of it, I was changing the conversation. "Remember I asked you who you had feelings for?"

Oliver focused on his food, taking a big bite of his burger.

Apparently I wasn't the only one who didn't want to talk. "Well?"

He swallowed and said, "Well, what?"

It was now or never. "Who is she?"

He started to take another bite of his burger but put it down. "You don't give up, do you?"

I smiled. "But this isn't about me wanting to know something. This is about me being your friend. You can talk to me, you know."

He took a sip of his Coke. "For the record, I never told her I loved her. It was Maggie. My wife's sister."

I leaned back in surprise. I hadn't expected him to answer me, and I certainly hadn't expected this to have anything to do with his wife. "Your wife's sister?"

"You know Jennie disappeared, right?" He spoke in a low, quiet tone. "Maggie and Jennie were only a couple of years apart, so they were close. But at the end, Jennie wasn't close to anyone."

I waited while he vanished into his head, reliving his memories of a woman he'd once loved. The story flashed through my mind while I waited for him to say more. No wonder he was having difficulty talking about it; the whole thing was a nightmare. In his previous job, while on assignment for the DEA, somehow Oliver's cover had been blown. He ended up badly beaten and left tied up in a warehouse. An anonymous caller notified the DEA office headquarters in Phoenix and let them know where Oliver had been left.

But the worst part was that while Oliver was being held captive, someone broke into his home and kidnapped his wife. She was never found.

"Maggie calls me occasionally. I don't encourage it, but she's never lost touch with me. We've known each other forever. Went to the same high school."

"The three of you were in school together?" I wanted to hear more about his past.

The waitress came over to check on us. We assured her we were fine, and she left. Oliver continued. "We hung out all the time. Jennie liked to tease me and say her little sister had a crush on me." He shrugged. "I never cared, but I was careful not to hurt her feelings. I didn't want to be a jerk."

"It sounds like she wants a relationship with you now." Which was weird since nobody knew what had happened to Jennie. *Maggie knows something.*

"She does. She always has. She called me from Mexico because her private investigator turned up a lead on Jennie. She wants me to come to Mexico." He rubbed his hand over his eyes.

I imagined if his wife were discovered alive, Oliver would return to his previous life out west. My stomach felt funny. "Are you going to Mexico to see what she's found?"

"No," he said. "The thing is, I don't believe it."

I didn't get it. "Don't believe what?"

"I don't believe the private investigator found a lead. Maggie's trying to drag me out there to convince me to be with her. She says she's been searching for Jennie, but I don't know. It doesn't sit right."

"It makes sense for her to look for her sister."

"That's not the part that gives me a bad feeling." He wadded up his napkin and tossed it on his empty plate. "Right before everything happened, Maggie made a pass at me. Not once, but three or four times. I told her no, of course, and I told Jennie about it, but I downplayed it. I didn't want the two of them fighting. But Jennie didn't care. She laughed it off. She'd say things like, 'go ahead, I don't mind.' I started to think she wanted me to say yes to Maggie."

Not good. "That doesn't make sense."

Oliver looked sober. "I don't think she wanted to be my wife. And I'm not sure she's missing."

I stared at him and decided to take a chance with what I knew. "You mean kind of like Joe isn't really missing?"

He fiddled with his napkin before leaning back. "Yes. The difference is that I think Joe is innocent."

Chapter Thirty-Three

The next day, I cleaned my apartment and tried not to think about Oliver and the situation with his wife. Instead, I mulled over what happened to Quinn and Valdorn and why Joe was afraid. I concentrated better when everything around me was organized, so I vacuumed, dusted, polished, and straightened.

Joe had counseled me to use my gift, but he was delirious. Use my gift in what way? How did he know I wasn't gifted with a big imagination? I didn't like the idea of going back into a shaman-trance.

It seemed multiple mysteries remained: Quinn and Valdorn's murders, who attacked Joe, and what the heck was Chase being investigated for? Two of those situations were tied to Stanley, who I no longer had any official reason to help, but my natural curiosity had taken over. Plus, the bitter part of me wanted to know if Stanley and his family were involved in any kind of criminal activity.

I poked through the refrigerator, checking expiration dates and planning my next meal. *That man is not to be trusted, not at all.* Win's words floated through my head. He might've been warning me about Stanley too. But I wasn't entirely convinced I could trust Win. Yes, he'd changed recently, but

Win Thurgood had yet to prove himself to be a stand-up guy.

My cell phone buzzed. I shut the refrigerator and grabbed the phone off the kitchen counter. "Hey, G, what's up?" I picked up a wipe to clean the counter.

"You are such a child."

How did crumbs get on my counter when I was never home? "Why am I a child?"

"Because you insist on shortening my name, despite my having asked you not to do that."

I stopped. He was right. My brother might be annoying at times, but he was my brother and deserved a level of respect. I'd been doing this for too long. "You're right. I'm sorry. It's a habit I got into, but I'll try to do better."

"Thank you." He sounded somewhat mollified. "Can you come into work tonight?"

I stopped wiping the counter. "Mom's there, isn't she?"

Giuseppe cleared his throat. "Yes. She's, ah, organizing things. Trying to help. You know, the usual."

"Sure. What time should I be there?" His actual request was to go in and hang around until after my mother left and put everything back the way my brother liked it.

"How about six? Then you don't have to wait too long for closing."

That gave me most of the day to finish up a few things. "Sure. Anything else you need?"

"Only the usual closing routine."

"You got it."

"Wait, one more thing." My brother took a breath. "Did you find Shaman Joe?"

Oh boy. I really didn't want to talk to my brother about this. Not because I thought he shouldn't know, but I was worried that he might tell the wrong person. Joe needed to stay hidden for now. I decided to go with

New-Age vague. "You know the universe presents answers when the time is right." I had no idea what the heck I was talking about, but it was the kind of thing my brother loved to hear.

"Absolutely," he breathed into the phone. "Ava, thanks. I knew I could count on you."

He hung up and I looked at the phone, baffled. Had I told him something I hadn't meant to tell him? I shook my head. Who knew.

I put my hands on my hips and surveyed the space. Everything was as clean as it was going to get. Sparky sat in front of me, ball in his mouth. It was time to play.

A section of woods in the northwest part of Brewster Square was great for hiking and hanging out. It was also a great place to spend time with my dog and my best friend, Charlie.

Charlie and I walked along a path as Sparky chased the ball I'd thrown. As long as I kept throwing the ball, he'd return to us. Charlie, determined to lose weight she didn't need to lose for the wedding, walked quickly along the path.

"It's a beautiful day," I noted. "You can enjoy the walk." She wore fire-engine red fitted workout clothes with a matching lightweight jacket. I would have looked like a tomato if I tried to wear that, but she looked great. I wore my usual black yoga pants and black t-shirt with gray running shoes.

"I've got a list of things to do a mile long. The wedding—I'm sorry. You don't want to hear about it."

"Why wouldn't I want to hear about the wedding? You're the one with the stress. All I have to do is enjoy the day when it comes."

She glanced sideways at me. "I thought this thing with Stanley would make it difficult."

"Stanley has nothing to do with you and Fred. It's fine. We weren't dating for long, anyway."

"I ran into Sydney at the grocery store yesterday."

I stiffened. "In the frozen foods aisle? Buying ice cream?"

Charlie shook her head. "No, sorry, produce section. Buying celery and carrots."

Rats. The ice cream aisle would've indicated higher odds of her and Stanley not speaking to each other. I did want Stanley to be happy. Just not with her.

"How are things with that family? Any news on the death?"

I deeply inhaled. "I have something to tell you." Charlie was silent while I filled her in on finding Joe. "You can't tell anyone, though. He's in hiding for a reason. We can't blow his cover."

"You trust this guy?" Charlie looked worried, a natural reaction. I would've been too if I didn't know Joe.

I nodded and tried to catch my breath as Charlie motored along the path. I wasn't sure this qualified as walking, as it felt more like we were almost running. "Slow down," I whined. "I'm curious about something Win said."

My words had the desired effect, and Charlie slowed her pace. "Oh lord, don't take that man seriously." She made a face. "He's interested in what's good for Win, not you or me. Did he say something mean to you? Because even though he seems to have changed, I'm not entirely convinced."

I wasn't either, but this wasn't the time. "Something he said related to Chase. He said Chase wasn't to be trusted. Do you know why he'd say that? I thought they were friends." I didn't actually know that they were friends, but I wondered if Charlie knew anything about Chase's job issues. It had nothing to do with all the other stuff going on, but I hated missing parts of a picture.

Charlie thought for a moment and shook her head. "I'm sorry, I have no idea. He has so many acquaintances and business associates, it's hard to keep them all straight. I never understand why he's friends with one person but not another. It all comes down to some sort of political maneuvering, but who knows? Did Joe say anything about any of this?"

"He said I have a gift and I have to use it."

Charlie nodded. "For what it's worth, I think he's right."

Sparky dropped the ball at my feet, and when I picked it up, I threw it in the opposite direction. "I know what I have to do."

When I walked into the gym this time, I didn't get such a cold reception. A couple of guys working out grunted at me, which I took as a form of hello. One of the kids yelled, "Yo, Coach, that lady is here again."

A nice turn of events. They'd realized I wasn't such a bad person and only trying to help.

"You remember," the kid yelled again, "the one with the stick up her—"

"Enough," Mr. Muscle said as he came out from his office. "Focus on what you're doing," he told the kid, who smirked at me. Mr. Muscle didn't look thrilled to see me, but he didn't immediately kick me out, either. He did, however, turn and walk back into his office.

I waited.

Joe came out minutes later. "Ava, great to see you again." An intent gaze emanated from his kind eyes. "What is your purpose today?"

"The same as every day, Joe. I'm here to find the truth."

He nodded. "Shall we take a journey?"

What did I have to lose? "Absolutely. But I need to be back at my brother's store by six."

Chapter Thirty-Four

What was I thinking? Just because some guy thought I had a gift didn't mean either of us was sane. But I liked Joe. I trusted he had my best interests at heart. Hell, I felt like he had the entire world's best interests at heart. He'd be able to help me tap into something in my subconscious. Perhaps I already knew the answer, and this could—

"Ava, are you ready?" Joe's hypnotic voice cut into my thoughts as I tried to get comfortable on the rickety folding chair. "Would you prefer to sit on a blanket on the floor?"

Eeeewwww.

Joe's eyes glinted. "I don't blame you. Do you remember what we did at the workshop?"

"Kind of. You started with a rattle?"

"We're going to skip that. You don't need it. I'm going to begin drumming, and that's when you'll find your entrance to the Lowerworld." I found his intensity a little unnerving. He pulled his chair close to mine. "Ava, I know something powerful happened last time you journeyed. You received a message related to what's going on right now. Pay attention, and we'll talk about what you see when you come back. I'm right here, and nothing can harm you."

I hadn't thought anything could hurt me until he said it. I worried. "Do bad things happen in the under—I mean, Lowerworld? It's my imagination, right?"

"You'll be fine." I hated non-answers, but I might as well push through and see what happened. He reached into a gym bag on the floor next to him and took out the same drum I'd seen him use at the workshop.

"Where'd you get that, anyway?"

"It was gifted to me by a medicine man," he said. He steadied his eye contact. "Remember, when it's time to return, I'll increase the tempo. Come back then. No lingering. Ready?"

I took a deep breath and centered myself. The drumbeat washed over me as I recreated my last journey through the tree. Once again, I dove inside the old oak, swooshed down a long, twisting slide, and landed in some sort of muck. The scent from the muck was like food left sitting in the sun: rotten.

Great. I hoped my pants in real life weren't as dirty as they were in this other place. I wiped my gooey hands on my shirt and tried to breathe through my mouth. It amazed me, whatever this journey thing was that I was doing. It seemed so real. Solid. I swiveled around to take it all in.

Things were different. It was the same place, but everything drooped a little, and the profusion of trees and plants sagged as if they needed water.

Or truth, a voice whispered.

What the hell?

They're killing us.

Creepy. A flash of intuition rippled through my mind. What was it Joe had said at the workshop? *"Each of us has a purpose on this planet, and we must recognize what we're here to do."* I knew I'd find my purpose here.

The trees towered over me and leaned slightly, as if pulled by gravity back to the ground. The colors of the landscape were muted, not nearly as vibrant as I remembered. Darkness closed in, a tangible presence that reminded me of the goo I'd landed in.

I studied the black goo covering my hands and clothes. What caused it? Was it my imagination or something more sinister at work?

She's back. She's back. She's back.

The frantic whispers around me cried, but once again, I couldn't figure out where they came from. I looked for signs of animals but found none. Not even the dog-like creature, the not-Sparky.

"I'm here," I yelled into the wilting forest. "What do you need?"

An answering groan raised the hairs on my arms. *They have killed many of us. Many of us. Their plan will kill us all.*

I started jogging, hoping to find someone or something who could help me. In the distance, a shimmering image of a dog took shape. I came closer. The not-Sparky sat beside a tall, thin man with wispy brown hair and a long beard.

"What's happening?" I asked.

"We thank you for making the journey," he said. "We have waited for you. Please know you're welcome here in our home at any time."

"Thank you. Can you tell me what I need to know?"

He began walking away with not-Sparky. "It's never that simple," he called over his shoulder.

I ran to catch up to him before he disappeared. "Why not? Tell me."

"That's not how it works here," he said. "We are governed by different forces and cannot be as direct as you might wish. We can guide you, but we cannot interfere."

I thought about it. "So, you can give me clues, but I have to figure things out for myself?"

A smile lit his face, and not-Sparky yipped. "Let's go!"

And with that, they broke into a run. "Hey!" I yelled. I chased them, losing direction as I did so. We ran through the woods for an indeterminate time; plants and trees drifted out of my way as I approached. I stumbled into a clearing where both man and not-Sparky stood in the center, waiting. Next to them were others, creatures part human and part animal. One woman, with long glimmering hair and the body of a horse, gazed at me with such love it took my breath away. Another woman, who I couldn't see clearly because she was fading, stood with tears streaming down her face. Some of the men stared at the ground, radiating grief.

Holy cannoli, what is this place?

I recognized the clearing from before. The mound in the center pulsated with an urgency that propelled me forward. Something was buried there, and it was my job to release it.

Without hesitation, I darted into the center of the clearing and began clawing at the ground. I was overtaken by frenzied scooping and digging as sweat poured down my face and time sped up. I reached into the hole I'd made and pulled out a white kitten. But there were more. I set the kitten aside and moved to the next area. I scraped and dredged until I pulled out a baby otter, slick and crying. I set him aside, moving on. Each time I dug, I pulled a baby out of the earth, and each time it was a different species. Kitten, otter, elephant, human. All the babies. All buried in the earth and unable to breathe. There wasn't enough time. I had to get them out. And then came the butterflies and the bugs. All buried. All dead.

Gogogogogogogogogogogogo...

It felt as if I'd been yanked by the top of my head and plunked back into reality. I opened my eyes slowly, aware of a heavy, aching feeling in my chest, as if I were getting sick.

When my eyes were fully opened, I stared directly into Joe's worried face. I guessed he had good reason to be worried, since the prep boys, Gavin and Pierce, stood behind him, not looking happy.

Chapter Thirty-Five

The last time something like this had happened to me, when I had been trapped by someone crazy, I'd had a ghost to back me up. Neither Quinn nor Valdorn was going to appear in their specter forms to help me; Valdorn didn't even like me when he was alive, and Quinn didn't really know me, so why should they help me now?

I tried to catch Joe's eye, but he seemed frozen. I tried to send him a psychic message. *Hello? Can you hear me?* He didn't look my way. So much for the psychic thing.

Gavin and Pierce glared at Joe, lips curled and sneering. "Did you think we wouldn't find you? If Nancy Drew here could do it, what made you think we couldn't?" Gavin said. "If only you'd stayed put so we could've finished you off that night like we finished Quinn."

"Shut up," Pierce said, almost pleasantly. "You're talking too much." He continued speaking in a congenial tone, sending chills through my body. "I'm going to need you both to stand in the corner. Put your arms around each other, so when you die, it'll look like two lovers committing suicide."

Was this guy serious? Suicide? "That's the dumbest thing I've ever heard," I said.

Pierce raised an eyebrow at me and gave a half-smile. "And why is it dumb, sweet Ava?"

Calling me "sweet Ava" was plain creepy. *You just came from the Lowerworld, and you're afraid of this guy?* His mannerisms and facial expressions sparked recognition. He was like the goo I'd landed in, sleazy and oozing with smelly gunk.

"How do you plan to kill us?" I asked, belligerent. I didn't like Pierce. Pierce was the dangerous one. He reached into his pocket, and I tensed, waiting for a gun.

Instead, he pulled out a bottle of pills. "You'll take these and die in each other's arms. It'll be perfect."

"That doesn't make sense. We're not a couple, so why would we do that?" I spoke before thinking. Why was I helping him plan my death? Not a good move. "And our friends out there aren't going to let you get away with this." Even if the kids in the boxing gym didn't like me or my corrections to their grammar, they wouldn't let us die in here. At least I didn't think they would.

"The door is locked," Gavin said, waving his arm backward and doing a weird hopping thing. His eye twitched, and he looked peculiar. *Is he high?*

"What's wrong with you?" I asked. "Are you high or something?"

Joe finally shook himself. "Ava, I don't think—"

Pierce laughed. "Or something. Don't worry about my friend. And don't worry about my plan. The details aren't going to matter to you. Now sit over there."

"No!" Joe's voice boomed over us. I looked at him in surprise. He wasn't messing around.

"Glad you're with me," I muttered.

"Sorry," he said. "I went somewhere when I pulled you out. I understand more now."

"Joe, glad to hear it. But we need to…" I didn't know what we needed to do except stay alive.

"You need to go sit over there and stop screwing around." Anger suffused Pierce's face. "I don't have time to waste. I've got a plane to catch."

"Going back to South America?" Joe was almost snide. Not the best approach, but what did I know?

"I have to do this work myself since you weren't any help."

"Is that why you got rid of Quinn?" Joe spat. "Because he was no use to you anymore? You have no respect for life."

Pierce laughed. "I have respect for money, which is what Quinn helped me get. But we had a larger vision, and he was no longer a part of that. It's too bad he couldn't find a way to help us, or he'd be the one dealing with the mess you've made."

"It took me a while to figure out what you were doing, and I don't appreciate you trying to use me for your criminal activities." Joe was mad, which surprised me. I assumed he was always calm and Zen-like, but I suppose anyone pushed far enough would be angry.

Gavin hopped around the office, shaking his head. "He knows, he knows, he knows," he said in a singsong voice. "That means he must die."

Pierce turned to Gavin. "Just because it's in your head doesn't mean you should say it." He sighed and turned back to us. "You two are loose ends, and loose ends get in the way of our revenue stream. We wouldn't want that, would we?"

I kind of thought we would want that. I leaned toward Joe and asked in a low voice, "Where's Mr. Muscle?"

"Don't worry about him," Pierce snarled. "He's where he needs to be."

"Did you read a handbook on how to be a villain?" I asked. "Because you couldn't be more clichéd if you tried."

"Shut. Up!"

I wasn't going down without a fight. Guys like him pissed me off, men who thought they could take whatever they wanted and get away with it.

Guys who might be handsome but were snakes. Guys who had different girlfriends all over the place, and none knew about each other. Just… guys. "Listen, you. You can't tell me what to do or how to die. You can't make me do anything I don't want to do. And you can't—"

"Aaaaayyyyyyyyyyyyyaaaaaaahhhhhhhhh!"

Everybody froze at the sound of the wail on the other side of the door, followed by a loud cracking noise.

"Yaaaaaahhhhhhhhhhhh!" The door banged open against the wall. A snarling woman dressed in a voluminous, white-feathered purple cape and pointy black witch's hat burst into the office. "Step away, or I shall curse you all," she yelled.

Nothing about this day surprised me at this point. "Debbee, what are you doing?" I asked.

"I'm helping you," she said.

I narrowed my eyes. "I don't need your help."

"We might, actually," Joe whispered.

"We do not need her help," I enunciated.

"They want to kill us, Ava. The more help we get, the better off we are."

Debbee reached into her cape and pulled out a foot-long stick. "I summon the forces of—"

"Gun!" Pierce dropped to the floor.

"Stop it," I insisted. "You're not helping!"

Gavin rolled along the floor. "Are you high?" I demanded. "Because for the love of God, you need to get up off that dirty floor."

"I place a curse upon thine enemies who arrive to harm thee." Debbee swung her stick through the air.

"You'll poke someone's eye out," I said.

"Curse ye, curse ye, curse ye," she chanted.

Gavin and Pierce retreated to a corner of the room, close to the bathroom door. I didn't blame them. I wanted to get away from her too. As she raised her hands to the heavens, Mr. Muscle and a few of the young boxers crowded near the broken door. "What the hell is going on in here?" Mr. Muscle yelled. "Someone tried to—"

"Freeze!" Oliver yelled behind Mr. Muscle. The police swarmed in, weapons drawn.

"Oliver!" Finally, someone who wasn't insane. Besides Joe and I, of course.

Joe blew out a breath and sat in one of the rickety chairs, dropping his head into his hands. "How did all this happen?"

"It worked, it worked!" Debbee yelled. "I saved Ava!"

"You didn't. You caused chaos and made everyone think you were going to shoot them with a stick." She smiled at me, smug. "Which is ridiculous since you probably picked up the stick outside right before you came in here." Her smile faded, and I felt bad. I didn't have to be so mean.

"Gavin Prescott and Pierce Coates, you're under arrest!" Oliver thundered.

The room fell silent. Everyone looked at each other. I checked the floor, remembering Gavin's weird rolling around stunt. The bathroom door stood slightly ajar. I looked at Oliver and inclined my head toward the bathroom. He nodded at me and gave a silent command to the officers in the room. Two approached the doorway, guns drawn, and rushed in there.

Nothing. No squeals of capture, no standoff. The officers came out shaking their heads.

"Window?" Mr. Muscle asked.

They nodded, and Oliver got on the radio, ordering people to do things in codes I didn't understand.

Debbee approached me and threw an arm around my shoulders. "You're safe."

I nodded, suddenly too tired from all of it. "Thanks."

She nodded back, solemn. "I had to right my karmic wrongs."

It was akin to making amends, so I accepted it. "I appreciate all your efforts to keep me safe."

"That's never an easy job," Oliver said, coming behind me. "Right now, I need you and Joe down at the station. We've got things to talk about."

CHAPTER THIRTY-SIX

She'd been following me around in a misguided attempt to help me,"
I explained to Giuseppe. We were in the shop, reviewing everything
that had happened and trying to figure out what it all meant.

"Righting the karmic balance," he said.

"The what?"

"She upset the karmic balance when she tried to kill you. She had to
reset the scales."

Whatever.

"Thanks for being here with me," I said, moving the candles back to the
middle and top shelf where they belonged (My mother insisted on putting
candles on the bottom shelves so people wouldn't buy them, in case they
burned their house down. Sometimes I completely understood her reasoning.
Not about the candles, though.). I'd told Giuseppe and my mother the entire
story when I arrived from the station earlier. Both listened, speechless. My
mother had a pained expression, as this was the second time this year that
her daughter had somehow gotten involved in events that almost ended
her life. She hugged me extra hard before she left, shaking her head and
muttering about having to be the one to tell my father.

Giuseppe stuck around to help fix the inventory chaos my mother had created. He didn't want to leave me alone, which was fine with me. Who knew what the criminal twins were up to out there or if they'd show up? Joe was in protective custody, but I had refused. I wasn't going to sit in some cell in the name of protection, even though Oliver told me I'd be in a safe house, not a cell. I had Sparky to take care of. Also, I didn't want to. The prep boys weren't going to turn my life upside down again.

From now on, no man would.

I hoped for a slow night, but the bell on the door tinkled, announcing someone's arrival. I sighed, moving the French Pear candle up a shelf between the French Lavender and Gingerbread.

"Can I help you?" Giuseppe asked stiffly.

My brother was always cheerful and pleasant to customers. I looked up at the tone in his voice, wondering why he sounded so annoyed.

"What a lovely little shop."

"Sydney, what are you doing here?" I asked, irritated that she existed.

"I'm here to shop. Isn't that why people come to this place?" She glided through the store, picking things up and putting them back down. "I've heard you have some charming knickknacks."

"I know exactly what you need," my brother said.

"Oh?" A look of disdain crossed her face as she sniffed the candles, acting as if I didn't exist.

"You need sage." My brother leaned forward and stage-whispered, "It will help with your little problem."

Sydney tilted her head to one side. "What problem? I don't have a problem."

Giuseppe nodded slowly. "You might not be aware of it, but it's clinging to you."

Suddenly apprehensive, Sydney looked behind her. "Can you get it off? What is it? Is it a spider? Please, can you get it off?"

My brother shook his head while I swallowed laughter. *Don't laugh, or you'll have to have your own version of righting karma to contend with.*

"The negativity is trapped in your aura, creating a disturbance in your kidney channel."

"What the hell are you talking about?" With one final look around, Sydney stomped out of the store.

"I hope we haven't upset the cosmos by doing that," I said.

My brother gave me an exasperated look. "Seriously? Haven't you learned anything by now?"

I smiled. "Nope."

Giuseppe smiled back. "As I thought. I'll smudge you later."

I laughed because I had no idea what he was talking about. "We should take a break. Mom left some brownies in the back. We don't want them to go bad."

"That would be a waste of Earth's resources," he said.

We found the brownies and proceeded to scarf them down. Giuseppe said around a mouthful of chocolate, "Hey, I have an idea about what was going on."

The sugar had worked its magic on me, and after the initial rush, I began to feel drowsy. "What are you talking about?"

"Those two criminals, the ones you called the prep boys. I know what they're doing."

Chapter Thirty-Seven

Maybe he did know something. My brother was a pretty intelligent guy. "It's all tied in with Joe somehow, and I'm pretty sure they killed Valdorn, too."

Giuseppe nodded. "Valdorn knew or saw things he wasn't supposed to know or see. I'm guessing they had to get rid of him. Like Quinn. Quinn and Valdorn are probably not the first people they got rid of."

"Nobody ever has to commit murder." I was angry and it came out in my tone. "I'm sorry, I'm not mad at you."

My brother tilted his head at me. "You said the same thing when Ethel was killed. You have a strongly developed sense of right and wrong."

"It's not hard," I said. "Murder is wrong; not killing someone is right. Cheating on your girlfriend by not telling her about your other girlfriend—that's wrong. Not cheating is right."

Giuseppe raised his hands in surrender. "You're preaching to the choir." He threw an arm around my shoulders. "And for the record, I'm sorry you had to deal with Stanley being a snot-gobbling dweeb."

I started laughing. "Eeeeewwww—and thank you for your support. But back to what you were saying. Do you have an idea about Valdorn's murder? What was he involved in that got him killed?" I pushed my plate away. Three brownies were enough. For now.

My brother didn't hesitate to answer. "Bugs." He stuffed another brownie in his mouth and waited for my reaction.

"That's…" I wanted to say crazy, but we'd shared a sibling moment, and I didn't want to undermine that. "…a thought," I finished. Was he referring to the bugs Gavin and Pierce had tried to sell him? "What do you mean by bugs?"

He swallowed and began pacing, warming to his subject. "Those guys at the gym were the same guys who came in here trying to sell me those gross bugs."

I'd already come to that conclusion. "You might be right, but I don't get how that leads to beating Shaman Joe and killing Quinn and Valdorn."

Giuseppe tapped his chin, deep in "thinker" mode. "What do the prep boys have in common with Joe and Valdorn and Quinn?"

I couldn't think of a strong connection. "They were all in this area at the same time? That's all I can think of."

My brother nodded. "True, and Valdorn and the prep boys knew each other, right?"

"Yes. They were here for that birding expo thing. And before you ask—" I held up a hand as if to stop him from saying anything. "All I know is that it's somehow related to bird species and migratory patterns, and that about covers it."

Giuseppe walked back to the front of the store and pulled out a notebook from behind the counter. "Here's our main players." He drew five small circles, one at each corner and one in the middle, and put an initial in each.

"What is PB1?" I asked. "Oh, wait. Prep Boy One." Sometimes the fact that I knew how my brother thought was scary. "Now connect those two to the V circle. And the V circle to the J circle. And Q to the PB's, I think."

We sat in silence, staring at our artistic masterpiece. Finally, I said, "Let's use our online ninja skills."

"You mean Google?"

"I mean Google. What should we use as our search terms?"

We went to the back office and started typing things in. The search *bugs for sale* brought up several bug kits and a variety of stock, including bugs, beetles, cockroaches, ants, and all sorts of creatures that made me itch.

"This all looks legal," I said. "Let's add the word 'illegal.' That'll change our results."

One little word made a huge difference. "Holy crow," Giuseppe whispered. "There's a whole world of people selling these things."

I was stunned. According to what I read on the screen, importing insects and arthropods, including scorpions, spiders, and millipedes, without a permit from the US Fish and Wildlife Service was asking for big trouble. It turned out the illegal wildlife trade was a multi-billion-dollar industry. "Giuseppe, it says 'illegal wildlife trade.' That means rhino horns."

"Disgusting," he interrupted.

"And birds," I continued. "Like the kind Stanley, his father, and Valdorn went and listened to lectures on. Birds and butterflies." I stopped, remembering something Chase had said. "I think the prep boys even presented at that thing."

"What does that mean?" Giuseppe asked, picking up his paper and connecting the circles.

"Let's look up *bug criminal.*"

"Why?"

"Why not?" I tossed back. "Who knows what we'll find?"

Several things turned up: how insects are used in forensic investigations; a gangster named Bugs Moran; and bug smuggling. Giuseppe shuddered. "That cannot be a thing."

"Oh yes it can," I said, skimming the article. *Wait, Queen Alexandra.* The largest butterfly on the planet was ripe for smuggling.

The bell on the door tinkled. I minimized the screen and got up to perform my retail duties. Giuseppe grabbed my arm, stopping me from leaving the office. "I'll get this," he growled.

"Can I help you?" he boomed, stepping into the store.

A hesitant voice stopped as my brother stood with his arms crossed.

A tingling started at the base of my scalp. I couldn't let him do this alone. "Debbee, what brings you here?" I asked, moving next to my brother.

"I told you to stay in the office," he stage whispered.

"No, actually you said you would get this." I turned and faced Debbee, knowing the direct method was best. "What's up?"

Her face was beet red, but she managed to continue to look me in the eye. "I want to apologize. Again. I'm sorry. I felt like I had to do something to make up for being so horrible to you before. I only wanted to help. I'll stay out of your life now."

As far as apologies go, hers wasn't too bad. She really was trying, and she had been trying on several occasions. "I appreciate your efforts," I said. "And you don't have to do anything else to prove your sincerity. I accept your apology."

A smile lit her face. "Really? Thanks! That's great! I mean—you know I'm on my medication, right? And I wouldn't normally kill anyone, right? This is so great. Thank you!" She giggled with giddy relief. "It sucks that those guys got away today, but at least I stopped them from hurting you, right? Hey, wanna get some coffee and talk about it?"

Oh boy. I didn't want to get some coffee and talk about anything, but I had to tread carefully here. "The police don't want us discussing the case," I suggested. "These guys are dangerous." In this instance, I wasn't fabricating the truth. "If they thought we were on their trail or anything, that might not be so good for us."

Giuseppe stepped forward as if to shield me. "I don't want my sister getting hurt again."

Debbee nodded. "You're right. Let's get together next week, instead, when all this is cleared up." She looked at me, and for a moment, she seemed especially young. "Again, I'm sorry."

"Thank you, Debbee. Have a great night," I answered. Oddly enough, I meant it.

Chapter Thirty-Eight

I'm not sure what woke me first, the pounding on my door or Sparky dropping a toy on my head. The hard plastic toy, not the stuffed one. "Hang on, buddy," I said, rolling out of bed. "I'm coming!" I went to the bathroom and put my curls up in a ponytail, swished mouthwash for half a second, and then went to the door.

Oliver held a takeout cardboard tray with two coffees and a bag of something that smelled delicious. "Breakfast delivery." His smile made me glad I'd used the mouthwash. He put the coffee and bag on the dining room table. "The coffee is black, so you can add whatever you want to it. I wasn't sure what you liked."

Sparky danced around with a tug toy in his mouth, and Oliver bent down to play for a moment. I cleared my throat. "Thank you. This is wonderful." I went to the kitchen to get plates. "What's in the bag?"

"Croissants. Plain. I thought of getting you chocolate but wasn't sure that would be suitable first thing in the morning."

And on what planet is chocolate not suitable in the morning? Yeesh. I placed the plates on the table, and we sat down. "I don't want to appear ungrateful, but I have a feeling you're not here to share a meal with me.

Has something happened?"

"We caught one of the guys who went after you at the gym."

My breath caught. "One of them?"

Oliver smiled. "Don't worry; I'm sure we'll catch up with the other one soon. It's too bad. Those guys had a lot going for them—smarts, education, looks—but they chose to throw away their lives. Gavin, who was high as a kite, had returned to their apartment over the coffee shop, and we caught him in possession of a number of illegal—"

"Don't tell me," I interrupted. "Bugs."

"Yep. I'll tell you about it, but first I'm going to use your bathroom and wash my hands." He nodded at Sparky on his way to the bathroom. "I don't want dog hair on my food." Sparky gave a short huff and lay in the center of the room.

I took the lid off one of the coffees, but before I could add anything to it, there was another knock at my door. My aunts must still be sleeping. Why was there so much traffic in my tiny apartment this early on a Wednesday morning? If it was Stanley, as I suspected, at least Oliver was here. That would make it easier to get rid of my ex.

I opened the door, and Pierce pushed me inside. "Bitch," he snarled. "You ruined things, but I'm fixing that. I thought about letting you go—"

"An excellent thought," I interrupted. "You should."

"Shut up!" he yelled, spittle flying from his mouth. He grabbed my forearms and started shaking me. "You and Joe screwed it up. All he had to do was one little job, one little trip to South America, but no, he has morals. Principles. When I'm done with you, I'm going to finish him, too."

Sparky launched at him, barking and snarling. "Sparky, down," I commanded, and to my relief, he obeyed. "Joe didn't do anything. He wasn't involved in your little criminal enterprise."

Pierce laughed. "No, and that's unfortunate for him. There's nothing little about our business. We make quite a good living. And although your *shaman* declined to help us, we'll find others who can source what we need."

"Butterflies, birds, and bugs?" I asked. "You kill creatures so you can make money." An image of digging babies from the earth came to me from my shamanic journey.

His grip on my arms tightened. "We started with the bugs, but you know, since we're such good businessmen, it's all about diversification, right? Birds and butterflies will bring us so much more money."

"You dig them up and rip them from their mothers." I twisted my arms from his grip and shoved his chest. Zero effect, but I was so mad I didn't care. "You're vile. You don't get to traffic things because you see a profit."

His face distorted in anger as he grabbed my arm again and wrenched it behind my back. "I'm done listening to you." He spun me around so I was facing my door and wrapped his arm around my neck. "This is going to be one of my most satisfying deaths."

Nothing can stop a person in their tracks faster than the sound of a gun cocking. *Click.* "Let. Her. Go."

Pierce let go and stepped back from me, arms in the air. I turned to face him, gulping air. Oliver grabbed his arm, twisted it behind his back, pulled a pair of cuffs out, and handcuffed him in one fluid motion.

"Impressive," I said.

He looked up at me. "You don't seem worried."

I smiled. "I knew you'd come out of the bathroom eventually. Want me to call your office?"

He snorted. "My office. Good one. I'll call this in and have patrol come get him."

Chapter Thirty-Nine

I remembered from experience that the booking process would take forever, so I waited for Oliver. I knew he'd be back. And even though I'd recently cleaned my apartment thoroughly, I started again.

Vacuum, dust, straighten.

My phone rang. Charlie. Did she know? "Hey, what's up?"

"Tell me you're okay."

She knew. "I'm okay." I pulled on the vacuum cleaner cord so it would retract and wheeled it to the closet. "Really, I'm fine. Oliver was here, so it all worked out. How did you know?"

"I was at the coffee shop and all the police went running out of there. Kenny said he'd heard it on the scanner. I had a feeling it was you. Do you want to talk?"

"Can we talk later? I think Oliver will be here soon to update me."

We said our goodbyes, and I promised to catch up with her later and tell her everything.

I had a lot to think about, including wildlife trafficking and the nature of shamanic journeys. What was real, and what was produced by my imagination? Did I need to differentiate, or could I chalk the whole thing up to one more experience that didn't need defining? I supposed I could draw a line between what I'd seen in my journey and what was happening, but did it matter? I had no interest in more shamanic journeys, no matter what Joe said.

I was relieved that the prep boys had been caught, and I wanted nothing more than for them to rot in a jail cell somewhere. It was bad enough that we—all humans—end up inadvertently hurting others during our everyday lives. But to purposefully harm other living things was vile. There are worlds within our world, and I'd come to believe that each part of our world depended on the balance that existed between everything.

But how did we maintain that balance when others, like Pierce and Gavin, were bent on destroying everything? People like Oliver and Joe and my brother and Charlie and my parents and aunts all had something in common. A deep, abiding sense of goodness. I couldn't picture Charlie ever hurting someone for personal gain; it wasn't in her DNA. What made the prep boys different? What made them kill without regard for how it affected other people, other lives?

I shuddered, remembering the scene in my apartment. After the police had hauled Pierce away, Oliver gazed at me in silence for a moment. "That could've gone very differently," he said.

I nodded. A mixture of feelings welled up inside me: anger, grief, despair. "Why did they do this?"

Oliver sighed. "Because they're the bad guys."

"Don't be flippant. It's not that simple."

"It is that simple. We've been watching these guys for a while."

"We?"

Oliver nodded. "The feds contacted me months ago. Gavin and Pierce ran an insect-smuggling operation and made tons of money. But they wanted more money; they always do. When they encountered resistance, they simply killed people who got in their way. I'd say that's kind of the definition of a bad guy."

"Everything they did was horrible, but I don't understand why. Why did they kill Quinn?"

Oliver shook his head. "Quinn was a liability. He wanted in on their enterprise, but he didn't have the overseas contacts to make it happen. They were going to cut Quinn out of the business, and he threatened to go to law enforcement. So they got rid of him. Remember, they were poised to make millions more off the bird and butterfly smuggling."

Something about it didn't sound right to me. "Why did they tell you this? How do you know that's how it happened?"

"They aroused suspicion last year, after a trip to Columbia, where lots of wildlife gets smuggled. Besides, Gavin is a stoner who can't keep his mouth shut."

I laughed. "Now it sounds right."

Oliver looked at his watch. "I've got to do some paperwork. Those other agencies always make things complicated. I'll come back in an hour or so and check on you."

I finished cleaning. Oliver would come over or, at the very least, call soon. I stood at my window and looked out over the town green, gazing at the collection of people and buildings that made this place my home. I loved it here, and I'd always fight to keep the bad guys from winning.

A knock on the door pulled me out of my reverie. "Who is it?" I asked.

"It's us. We need to make sure you're alive and kicking."

I pulled open the door and let my aunts in, all of them. Claudia and Estelle, who had been partners forever, rushed to hug me. Aunt Maria handed me a plate of cookies. Aunt Sophia and Aunt Ava went straight to my refrigerator and put things in there. This was my lucky day for food. "I'm fine, I promise. Do you want coffee? I can make a fresh pot."

Aunt Sophia shook her head. "No, thank you. We heard the commotion and needed to put eyes on you instead of talking on the phone. Besides, the hunky lawman is on his way up." She bent down and petted Sparky.

Simultaneously, they all began to edge their way out my door.

"The hunky lawman is hooking me up with a search and rescue training program for Sparky," I said.

"What hunky lawman?" Oliver stood at the top of the stairs, grinning at me.

I grinned back. "That's my aunt Maria's name for you."

"I call it like I see it," she said as all the aunts smiled, turned, and went downstairs, whispering to each other.

I beckoned him inside. "C'mon in. Everyone in jail where they belong?"

He came in and put a box of pizza on my kitchen table. "Everyone is exactly where they belong."

"More food? You already fed me once today. What's the occasion?"

"You need to eat. The food will ground you. You did have someone want to kill you for a second time today."

I opened the box to find a veggie pizza. "I have to ask you something that I haven't been able to understand."

"Of course you do." Oliver smiled and sat at the table.

I sat next to him and tried to put my thoughts in order. "So, Gavin and Pierce were selling bugs? And they made a lot of money, right?"

Oliver nodded. "It's a big business."

I stood and walked to my cabinet, got two plates, and came back to the table. "They wanted to sell birds and butterflies? They could hide the butterflies easily enough, but birds?"

"It's complicated," Oliver said, taking a slice of pizza. "But yes, birds can be hidden in all kinds of things. Toilet paper rolls, curlers. This new enterprise of theirs was one of the reasons they've been networking within certain circles, and it's why they were at the conference. We've been working with the feds on this, and it seems they'd already made some contacts in the smuggling world. The illegal butterfly trade is a 200-million-dollar industry."

"What?" That number astounded me.

"The agent I've been working with told me that even though climate change has affected a huge number of species and caused extinction, the illegal trade has brought about the demise of species as well."

My vision swam. "We've killed entire species for money?" The scent of the pizza made me slightly nauseous.

"Rare butterflies sell for more than $10,000 each."

"Like Queen Alexandra's Birdwing?"

"Exactly." Oliver folded his pizza and took a large bite. Still trying to process what he was saying, I left mine on the plate. "In some parts of New York, they have finch-singing contests and the winning bird earns a cash prize. Because of things like that, people smuggle birds into the country. Some guy at an airport was recently caught smuggling finches; he'd hidden them inside hair curlers." Oliver wiped his face, finished with his slice of pizza. He stood and went to the front window, looking out at the town.

I shook my head. "That's insane."

"Birds are sold to collectors, taxidermists, people who want them as pets, and sometimes even people who want to eat them."

I didn't know what to say. The entire issue made me profoundly sad.

Oliver walked back to the table, reached over, and grabbed another slice of pizza. "Are you and Stanley over?" he asked around a mouthful of cheese.

"Yes, why?" I didn't want to get into it, but I'd answer whatever questions Oliver had.

"Because his father is here," Oliver said. "I saw him walking across the Green to your front door just now."

Crap. He did sort of hire me to find Valdorn, which I'd failed miserably at.

"It's not your fault the hippie died," Oliver said as he wiped some tomato sauce off his chin. "Don't let him make this your fault."

"You told me that he'd been suspended from teaching at the college. Do you know why?" Not that it mattered at this point, but I liked to know the final answers.

"He allegedly took some bribes from parents who wanted their kids to have good grades."

Holy crow. The birdman was corrupt. "I wonder what he wants from me."

"Do you want me to talk to him and tell him to leave?"

"No, I can handle it," I said with resignation. If I could handle the prep boys, this should be a piece of cake. My phone rang, and I answered. "Stanley's dad?" I asked. "Got it in one," my aunt replied.

Oliver threw his napkin in the garbage. "I'm going back to the station to finish more paperwork. Call me if Chase gives you a hard time."

I could deal with Stanley's father and whatever he had to say. Oliver walked out my door and stood on the landing for a moment, talking with Chase at the top of the stairs. When Oliver left, Chase hovered in the doorway. "You can come in," I said.

He walked in subdued, as if he had been chastised for something, and gently closed the door. "I'm sorry to bother you. I know you've been through a lot this week. I wanted to have a brief chat before I left." He hovered just inside the door.

I nodded and waited. We were no longer connected in any way. I wasn't dating his son, and the mystery he'd asked me to solve had been resolved. So what did he want?

"I wanted to explain a few things," he said.

People always want to explain themselves after something bad happens. A wave of fatigue washed over me. "I don't need to hear this. I'm not trying to be rude, but I don't think we have anything to talk about. Everything's been resolved, and you can go home now. I'm sorry Valdorn died, and I'm sure Tory's crushed, but I couldn't stop it." I picked up my pizza slice again and put it down.

Chase nodded and took a few steps into the room. "Nobody expected you to stop a murder. I thought he was hiding out somewhere, smoking weed or something, or playing some kind of head game with my daughter. Nobody had any idea he was in danger."

Except for Tory. The thought popped into my head, but I pushed it aside. It didn't matter now.

"Well, have a good trip home."

"I don't have a job to go back to, you know."

I didn't take the bait. I knew the university had suspended him and I knew why, but it wasn't my business and I didn't want to have a conversation about it.

He kept talking and wandered toward my couch. "I doubt I'll get a job in academia again. It's time to retire. Time to get a new focus. What happened wasn't my fault, but they're blaming me anyway. There's always got to be a scapegoat, you know."

Scapegoat. It wasn't his fault. Like it wasn't Stanley's fault that Sydney was still in his life. Or like it wasn't Birdie's fault that she expected Sydney and Stanley to get married. I was tired of his family's blame-shifting and history rewrites. I stood. "Thank you for coming by. I have things to do, so you'll have to leave now." I worded it as politely as I could.

He looked a bit surprised but held out his hand. "It's too bad things didn't work out between you and my son, but I wish you nothing but the best. Good luck."

I shook his hand and gave him a small smile. As I watched him leave, I thought about how luck is often made and not something that just happens. Maybe that family would realize the truth of that someday. Or not.

Chapter Forty

Giuseppe and I had pretty much gotten the store back to its original state. My mother was helping Janine pack, as they were scheduled to close on their new house the next day, and she hadn't been around to rearrange things. I wondered if my mother was "helping" to pack the same way she helped at the store. What mattered was that my family was there for each other whenever someone needed help.

"G—um, Giuseppe, I'm going to put the new inventory on the shelves."

My brother smiled at me. "Thank you, and thank you for making an effort not to call me G."

I'd never considered that I was doing my brother an unkindness until recently. I took a breath. It was important that I treat everyone well and focus on being kind. I didn't know what made people like Gavin and Pierce the way they were; maybe it was genetics, or perhaps they had a crappy childhood, but I didn't ever want to be the reason someone got hurt. It was bound to happen unintentionally, but I'd do what I could to make the world a better place.

"You need to switch to a plant-based diet," my brother said. "Give up all those chemicals in things like pepperoni and store-bought bread."

"And you need to mind your business." So I was a work in progress. Not everything deserved kindness, and the food my brother ate fell into that category.

The bell over the door announced a visitor, and I glanced up from the packing list I had in my hand. I couldn't stop the smile that spread across my face.

"Ava." His gentle voice made me feel warm and safe, despite the weirdness we'd encountered together. Joe felt like another brother to me.

I raised a hand in a half wave. "Hey shaman, how's it going?"

Giuseppe came over and hugged him, doing that back-slap thing that guys do. "Good to see you, my friend."

He wore jeans and a loose t-shirt. "Are you here to say goodbye?" I asked.

"How did you know?"

I looked him up and down. "You're wearing comfortable clothes. Plus, you spend a lot of time traveling, so it would only make sense that you're off to your next adventure."

Joe laughed. "You'll be an excellent private eye."

I raised an eyebrow. "Is that a prediction?"

He shook his head. "Your brother told me you were thinking of it as a career."

I'd thought he might know my future, but that wasn't how it worked. Things were never that easy. "Have a safe trip. When will you be back?"

"I'll come back late summer or early fall. It kind of depends on a couple of things. I've got some work to do, though. I need to make sure that the people I work with are aware of the dangers of the outsiders."

"What?" Outsiders? Where was he going?

"I do specific work with tribes in South America," he clarified. "And this thing that happened with Gavin and Pierce made me realize how vulnerable some of the tribespeople are. I need to do what I can to protect them so they aren't taken advantage of. Those two aren't the only people who've tried to take what's not theirs."

"I expect it's a rising tide you're fighting," my brother said. "Everyone romanticizes the indigenous peoples. Even if you can help stop wildlife theft, cultural appropriation is a real problem."

Joe ran a hand through his hair. "It is. We do what we can, right?" Joe and Giuseppe were silent for a moment. "But anyway, I came by to see you and thank you again, Ava. Remember, you have a gift. Anytime you need to use it, it's there for you."

I shook my head. "I'm not doing that unless you're around. I'll wait for you to come back." I stepped forward and hugged Joe. "Please be careful. Call me when you return, and we'll get a pizza." My brother glared at me, so I amended my statement. "Or something healthy. A tofu dog or something."

He smiled and returned my hug. "Thank you, from me and the beings who couldn't speak for themselves. You helped save the creatures who have no voice."

I flashed back to the image from my journey, the image of all the buried babies. "You helped too, my friend."

Chapter Forty-One

Moving day arrived for my brother. The apartment over the store was packed up, and everyone hauled boxes and furniture out to the moving truck. It wasn't a long trip to his new home, but the moving truck was a must-have. We were well past the days of asking a friend who owned a pickup truck for help.

I waited while my father rearranged the interior of the truck. He sought to minimize the number of trips needed for the move. I estimated we'd need to go back and forth three times, but my brother insisted we could get it all in one.

He'd enlisted a couple of his friends from the ghost-hunting business to help. Charlie and Fred came to move boxes, and Oliver had shown up too. I knew one of the main reasons everyone had agreed to help, as it was no secret that my mother had lunch ready for everyone at the new house. If you fed them, they would come.

Except for Oliver. I wasn't sure if he was there because of the food or other reasons. He kept staring at me when he thought I wasn't looking, and it was starting to unnerve me. Finally, I confronted him. "What?" I demanded.

He tried to look innocent. "What?"

"Why do you keep staring at me?"

"What?"

"How eloquent for a law enforcement officer. Don't you have any other words you can use?"

"What, ma'am?" He tried to hide his smirk.

I threw a couch pillow at him. He ducked, but I managed to nail him with it. "Hey!" my brother yelled. "Careful with our stuff!"

"It's a pillow," Oliver and I yelled simultaneously.

"I don't want it getting dirty," Giuseppe said.

"Sorry," I said, properly chastised. I turned back to Oliver. "Seriously, is something wrong?"

"No, I'm looking forward to seeing the new house, that's all."

I narrowed my eyes at him. "That's all?"

He nodded with an air of complete innocence. "Oh look, your father was able to make more space on the truck."

"Stop right there." My voice could be commanding like my mother's when I needed it to be. Oliver froze. "Tell me the truth right now. What's going on?"

He sighed and drifted closer to me. "I'm curious," he hesitated. "I know from my experience with you that sometimes you… sometimes there are things… I know you can…"

"Oh, for God's sake, spit it out. We don't have all day."

My brother strode past us on his way to pick up more boxes. "I told him about your abilities. He wants to know if you'll see any ghosts today."

I glared at them both. "What abilities?"

Giuseppe shrugged and stopped by the back door. "I know you saw Ethel a few months ago, and Joe said you have special abilities when it comes to shamanic journeying. We wondered if you'd see Quinn back here."

I shuddered and looked first at the dumpster where Joe had been hurt and then where I'd found Quinn dead on the ground. "I don't see anything,"

I said. "Honestly. And I'm glad because it'd be distracting. Let's get the truck loaded."

About an hour later, the truck brimmed with as much as it could hold, and it was time to drive to the new house and start unloading. As I'd predicted (and wisely kept to myself), not everything fit in the truck.

Giuseppe and Janine's new house was on the west side of town. Our little caravan started driving up Chartres Drive, past the creepy house where Ethel died, to the fork in the road. Going left at the split would lead to my parents' house, but we went right, past the old warehouse where white wisps curled from the smokestacks. I had no idea what was there, but it was in use. I made a mental note to ask someone later.

A block down the road, opposite the warehouse, the cemetery came into view. I wasn't sure who took care of the place, but it was well manicured, not overgrown or haunted looking.

My brother's new house was right after we passed the cemetery. The sinewy driveway veered to the right after about 300 meters. The home faced south, so the front had a spectacular view of the gravestones.

Perfect for my brother and his family.

Everyone climbed out of their vehicles and stood quiet for a moment. "I'm happy for you," I said to Giuseppe and Janine. And I was. But also unsettled, because something about the house bothered me.

It was a large, rectangular building with white siding and no shutters. Built in a plain New England style, I guessed it was more than a century old. Oliver walked up and stood beside me. "This is nice," he said. "Big, too. It'll be great for you to have two whole floors to yourselves."

"Two and a half," Giuseppe said with pride.

I squinted, trying to see the half-floor, but failed. The steeply pitched roof probably hid something, I thought. I made out small dentil moldings below the cornice. A brick chimney rose from the center, and I counted nine windows at the front with a gabled hood over the door entry.

"Let's get started. We've got some work to do," my father called.

Everyone helped unload the truck, and when Janine opened the front door, we trekked inside, asking where to put things. "The kitchen is in the back," Janine called. "Bedrooms are upstairs. If you're unsure where the box goes, leave it in the dining room, which is on the right here. Ava, can you watch Baby Danny for a second? I'm going to show Oliver where to put the baby's things."

I dropped the box I carried onto the floor and held out my arms, happy to take my nephew since breakfast had happened quite a while ago. He smiled his sweet, goofy smile at me and snuggled in my arms.

"I haven't seen the upstairs yet," my mother said, and with that, everyone marched up the steps, talking all at once and leaving Baby Danny and me to fend for ourselves.

Suddenly fussy, Baby Danny squirmed in my arms until I put him down, and he immediately ran to the back of the house. *Crap. I forgot how mobile he is now.* I chased him to the kitchen, following close behind him. "Slow down, little man, your auntie's gonna catch you!"

"Leave the kid alone, lady. He's playing."

At the sound of the voice, a chill infused my body. I looked to my right. The man who stood there wore a dark pinstriped suit with a matching vest and red tie. His hat, a gray fedora, sat tilted on his head.

"No, oh no, no…" My words came out in a whisper.

"No what?" the man demanded.

"Just no," I said, my voice stronger. "You're not here." I had to say it because I knew what I was seeing couldn't be real. But it must be. There was no mistake.

I was seeing a ghost.

"Oh, I'm here alright, sweetheart," he said with a laugh. "Even my little buddy knows it." With that, he kneeled, and Baby Danny giggled and gave him a high five.

"What's going on in here?" Janine asked, swooping in and picking up my nephew. She walked right through the man in the fedora. "Are you two playing? Baby Danny loves it in the kitchen," she said.

"I'll bet he does," I said as my nephew tilted his head at me and smiled.

Coming Soon...

SEARCHING IN BREWSTER SQUARE

Ava and Sparky have joined the Connecticut Shoreline Search and Rescue team. But when training turns into a real-life problem, they'll have more to figure out than land navigation techniques.
Can Ava and her dog track down a killer who struck years ago, or has the trail gone cold?

About the Author

Narielle Living is a freelance writer based out of the tidewater area of Virginia. In addition, she is the editor of the Williamsburg magazine *Next Door Neighbors* and has written hundreds of do-it-yourself articles for online magazines. Her mysteries include *Signs of the South, Revenge of the Past*, and *Madness in Brewster Square*, and she co-authored *Chesapeake Bay Karma—The Amulet*. Her fiction also appears in the anthologies *Chesapeake Bay Christmas Volume I, Chesapeake Bay Christmas Volume II, Chesapeake Bay Christmas Volume III*, and *Harboring Secrets*. She edits both fiction and non-fiction, and loves helping other writers achieve their goals. Narielle is currently working on the next books in the Brewster Square series as well as other fun writing projects.

For information about her books or workshops, visit www.narielleliving.com or find her on Facebook Instagram, and Twitter.